Mrs. Frisby
and the
Rats of NIMH

Mrs. Frisby
and the
Rats of NIMH

Robert C. O'Brien
illustrated by Zena Bernstein

AN ALADDIN BOOK
Atheneum

TO *Catherine Fitzpatrick*

PUBLISHED BY ATHENEUM
COPYRIGHT © 1971 BY ROBERT C. O'BRIEN
PICTURES BY ZENA BERNSTEIN
ALL RIGHTS RESERVED
PUBLISHED SIMULTANEOUSLY IN CANADA BY
MCCLELLAND & STEWART, LTD.
MANUFACTURED IN THE UNITED STATES OF AMERICA BY
FAIRFIELD GRAPHICS, FAIRFIELD, PENNSYLVANIA
ISBN 0-689-70413-5

Contents

Mrs. Frisby
and the
Rats of NIMH

The Sickness
of Timothy Frisby

Mrs. Frisby, the head of a family of field mice, lived in an underground house in the vegetable garden of a farmer named Mr. Fitzgibbon. It was a winter house, such as some field mice move to when food becomes too scarce, and the living too hard in the woods and pastures. In the soft earth of a bean, potato, black-eyed pea and asparagus patch there is plenty of food left over for mice after the human crop has been gathered.

Mrs. Frisby and her family were especially lucky in the house itself. It was a slightly damaged cinder block, the hollow kind with two oval holes through it; it had somehow been abandoned in the garden during the summer and lay almost completely buried, with only a bit of one corner showing above ground, which is how Mrs. Frisby had discovered it. It lay on its side in such a way that the solid parts of the block formed a roof and a floor, both waterproof, and the hollows made two spacious rooms. Lined with bits of leaves, grass, cloth, cotton fluff, feathers and other soft things Mrs. Frisby and her children had collected, the house stayed dry, warm and comfortable all winter. A tunnel to the surface-earth of the garden, dug so that it was slightly larger than a mouse and slightly smaller than a cat's fore-leg, provided access, air, and even a fair amount of light to the living room. The bedroom, formed by the second oval, was warm but dark, even at midday. A short tunnel through the earth behind the block connected the two rooms.

Although she was a widow (her husband had died only the preceding summer), Mrs. Frisby was able, through luck and hard work, to keep her family—there were four children—happy and well fed. January and February were the hardest months; the sharp, hard cold that began in December lasted until March, and by February the beans and black-eyes had been picked over (with help from the birds), the asparagus roots were frozen into stone, and the potatoes had been thawed and refrozen so many times they had acquired a slimy texture and a rancid taste. Still, the Frisbys made the best of what there was, and one way or another they kept from being hungry.

Then, one day at the very end of February, Mrs. Frisby's younger son, Timothy, fell sick.

That day began with a dry, bright, icy morning. Mrs.

Frisby woke up early, as she always did. She and her family slept close together in a bed of down, fluff, and bits of cloth they had gathered, warm as a ball of fur.

She stood up carefully so as not to awaken the children, and walked quietly through the short tunnel to the living room. Here it was not so warm, but not really cold either. She could see from the light filtering down the entrance tunnel that the sun was up, and bright. She looked at the food in her pantry, a hollowed-out space lined with small stones in the earth behind the living room. There was plenty of food for breakfast, and lunch and dinner, too, for that matter; but still the sight depressed her, for it was the same tiresome fare they had been eating every day, every meal, for the last month. She wished she knew where to find a bit of green lettuce, or a small egg, or a taste of cheese, or a corn muffin. There were eggs in plenty not far off, in the hen house. But hens and hens' eggs are too big for a field mouse to cope with; and besides, between the garden and the hen-house there was a wide sward of shrubs and grass, some of it grown up quite tall. Cat territory.

She climbed up the tunnel, emerging whiskers first, and looked around warily. The air was sharp, and there was white frost thick on the ground and on the dead leaves at the edge of the wood across the garden patch.

Mrs. Frisby set off over the gently furrowed earth, and when she reached the fence, she turned right, skirting the border of the forest, searching with her bright round eyes for a bit of carrot, a frozen parsnip, or something green. But there was nothing green at that time of year but the needles on the pine trees and the leaves on the holly, neither of which a mouse—or any other animal, for that matter—can eat.

An then, straight in front of her, she did see something green. She had reached the far corner of the garden, and there, at the edge of the woods where it met the fence, was a stump. In the stump there was a hole, and out of the hole protruded something that looked a little like a leaf, but was not.

Mrs. Frisby had no trouble at all going through the cattle wire fence, but she approached the hole cautiously. If the stump was hollow, as it seemed to be, there was no telling who or what might be living in it.

A foot or so from the hole she stopped, stood still, and watched and listened. She could hear no sound, but from there she could see what the green was. It was, in fact, a yellowish-brownish-green: a bit of a corn shuck. But what was a corn shuck doing there? The cornfield was in a different part of the farm altogether, away beyond the pasture. Mrs. Frisby hopped closer and then, carefully, crept up the side of the stump and peered inside. When her eyes got used to the dark, she saw that she had found a treasure: a winter's supply of food, carefully stored and then, for some reason, forgotten or abandoned.

But stored by whom? A racoon perhaps? Not very likely, so far from the stream. More likely a squirrel or a ground hog. She knew that both of these felt free to help themselves to the new corn each year, and that they were strong enough to carry ears away and store them.

But whoever had done it, why had he then abandoned the store? And then she remembered. Back in November there had come from near that edge of the woods the sound that sends all of the animals in the forest shivering to their hiding places—the sound of hunters' guns shooting, the sound that is accompanied, for someone, by a fiery stabbing pain. And then he never needs his stored food again.

Still, since Mrs. Frisby did not even know what kind of animal it had been, much less his name, she could not shed many tears over him—and food was food. It was not the green lettuce she had longed for, but she and her children were extremely fond of corn, and there were eight large ears in the stump, a noble supply for a mouse family. Down under the corn she also could see a pile of fresh peanuts (from still another part of the farm), some hickory nuts, and a stack of dried, sweet-smelling mushrooms.

With her forepaws and sharp teeth she pulled off a part of the husk from the top ear of corn and folded it double to serve as a crude carrying bag. Then she pulled loose as many of the yellow kernels as she could easily lift, and putting them in the shuck-bag she hopped off briskly for home. She would come back for more after breakfast and bring the children to help.

She backed down the tunnel entrance to her house tail first, pulling the corn after her and calling cheerfully as she went:

"Children! Wake up! See what I have for breakfast. A surprise!"

They came hurrying out, rubbing their eyes in excitement, for any kind of surprise in food was a rare and festive thing in the cold dead of winter. Teresa, the oldest, came first; crowding close behind her was Martin, the biggest, a strong, quick mouse, dark-haired and handsome like his poor father. Then came Cynthia, the

youngest, a slim, pretty girl-mouse, light haired, and, in fact, a little light-headed as well, and over-fond of dancing.

"Where is it?" she said. "What is it? Where's the surprise?"

"Where is Timothy?" asked Mrs. Frisby.

"Mother," said Teresa, concerned, "he says he's sick and can't get up."

"Nonsense. Martin, tell your brother to get out of bed at once or he'll get no breakfast."

Martin ran to the bedroom obediently but came back in a moment alone.

"He says he feels too sick, and he doesn't want any breakfast, even a surprise. I felt his forehead, and it's

8

burning hot."

"Oh, dear," said Mrs. Frisby. "That sounds as if he really is sick." Timothy had, on occasion, been known to think he was sick when he really was not. "Here, you may all have your breakfast—save Timothy's—and I'll go and see what's wrong."

She opened up the green carrying bag and put the corn on the table, dividing it into five equal shares. The dining table was a smooth piece of lath supported on both ends by stones.

"Corn!" shouted Martin. "Oh, Mother. Where did you ever get it?"

"Eat up," said Mrs. Frisby, "and a little later I'll show you, because there's a lot more where this came from." And she disappeared into the little hallway that led to the bedroom.

"A lot more," Martin repeated as he sat down with his two sisters. "That sounds like enough to last till moving day."

"I hope so," Cynthia said. "When is moving day, anyway?"

"Two weeks," said Martin authoritatively. "Maybe three."

"Oh, Martin, how do you know?" protested Teresa. "What if it stays cold? Anyway, suppose Timothy isn't well enough?"

At this dreadful thought, so casually raised, they all grew worried and fell silent. Then Cynthia said:

"Teresa, you shouldn't be so gloomy. Of course he'll be well. He's just got a cold. That's all." She finished eating her corn, and so did the others.

In the bedroom Mrs. Frisby felt Timothy's forehead.

It was indeed hot, and damp with sweat. She took his pulse and dropped his wrist in alarm at what she felt.

"Do you feel sick to your stomach?"

"No, Mother. I feel all right, only cold, and when I sit up I get dizzy. And I can't get my breath too well."

Mrs. Frisby peered anxiously at his face, and would have looked at his tongue, but in the dark room she could see no more than the dim outline of his head. He was the thinnest of her children and had a dark complexion like his father and brother. He was narrow of face; his eyes were unusually large and bright, and shone with the intensity of his thought when he spoke. He was, Mrs. Frisby knew, the smartest and most thoughtful of her children, though she would never have admitted this aloud. But he was also the frailest, and when colds or flu or virus infections came around he was the first to catch them and the slowest to recover. He was also—perhaps as a result—something of a hypochondriac. But there was no doubt he was really sick this time. His head felt as if he had a high fever, and his pulse was very fast.

"Poor Timothy. Lie back down and keep covered." She spread over him some of the bits of cloth they used as blankets. "After a while we'll fix you a pallet in the living room so you can lie out where it's light. I've found a fine supply of corn this morning, more than we can eat for the rest of the winter. Would you like some?"

"No, thank you. I'm not hungry. Not now."

He closed his eyes, and in a few minutes he went to sleep. But it was a restless sleep in which he tossed and moaned continually.

10

In mid-morning Mrs. Frisby, Martin, and Cynthia set off for the stump to carry home some more of the corn, and some peanuts and mushrooms (the hickory nuts they would leave, for they were too hard for mouse jaws to crack, and too tedious to gnaw through). They left Teresa home to look after Timothy, whom they had wrapped up and helped into a temporary sickbed in the living room. When they returned at lunchtime, carrying heavy loads of food, they found her near tears from worry.

Timothy was much worse. His eyes looked wild and strange from the fever; he trembled continuously, and each breath he took sounded like a gasp for life.

Teresa said: "Oh, Mother, I'm so glad you're back. He's been having nightmares and shouting about monsters and cats; and when I talk to him, he doesn't hear me at all."

Not only was Timothy not hearing with his ears; his eyes, though wide open, were not seeing, or if they were, he was not recognizing what they saw. When his mother tried to talk to him, to hold his hand and ask him how he felt, he stared past her as if she did not exist. Then he gave out a long, low moan and seemed to be trying to say something, but the words would not form properly and made no sense at all.

The other children stared in frightened silence. Finally Martin asked:

"Mother, what is it? What's wrong with him?"

"He is terribly ill. His fever is so high he has become delirious. There is nothing for it—I will have to go and see Mr. Ages. Timothy must have medicine."

Mr. Ages

Mr. Ages was a white mouse who lived across the farm and beyond, in a house that was part of a brick wall. The wall lined the basement of what had once been a large farmhouse. The farmhouse itself had burned down so many years ago that nobody could remember what it had looked like nor who had lived there. The basement remained, a great square hole in the ground; and in its crumbling walls, protected from the wind and snow, numerous small creatures lived. In summer there were snakes, dangerous to Mrs. Frisby, but there was no need to worry about them in winter.

Just the same, it was a long, hard journey and could

be risky unless she was extremely cautious. It was so far, in fact, that Mrs. Frisby would not ordinarily have set out so late in the day, for fear that the dark would catch her before she got back. But Timothy obviously could not wait until the next day. So only five minutes after she had announced that she must go, she was gone.

If she had been able to follow her nose, that is, to take the shortest route to where Mr. Ages lived, her journey would have been easy enough. But since that would have led her close to the farmhouse and the barn, and since the cat stalked those grounds relentlessly, she had to plot a much more roundabout way, circling the whole wide farmyard and sticking to the fringe of the woods.

She loped along briskly, moving in the easy, horse-like canter mice use when they are trying to cover ground. Her progress was almost completely noiseless; she chose her path where the earth was bare, or where grass grew, and she avoided dead leaves, which would rustle and crackle even under her small weight. Always she kept an eye out for hiding places—logs, roots, stones, things to scurry under if she should meet a larger animal who might be unfriendly. For though the cat was number one, there were other things in the woods that chased mice.

And as she did all this, she worried about Timothy and hoped that Mr. Ages would know something that would help him.

It was more than two hours later that she saw she was getting close to the brick wall where he lived. Though her husband had been a great friend of Mr.

Ages and had visited him often, Mrs. Frisby herself had been there only once before, and that had been in summer. Still, she remembered the place clearly. It was an odd sort of clearing in the woods. Long ago, when the old house had been lived in, before it had burned, there must have been a wide lawn around it. Over the years this clearing had grown over with a strange mixture of high, rank grass, tall weeds, berries and wild flowers. In the summer it was a wild and beautiful place, bright with blooms and full of the smell of blackberry blossoms and purple clover. There were harsher plants as well—spiked jimson weeds and poisonous dark pokeberries, and bees droning everywhere.

But in winter it had a bleak and almost ghostly look, for the blossoms and the green leaves were gone, and only the dry skeletons of the weeds stood, hung with stalks and seeds and pods that rattled in the wind. It was from these seeds and others, and from the flowers and roots beneath them, that Mr. Ages made the draughts and powders that could sometimes save the sick from dying.

The time she had been here before—that was for Timothy, too, when he was only a baby, scarcely bigger than a marble. He had wandered, while playing with the other children, a little way from them and had been bitten or stung by something poisonous. They did not know what. When the others found him, he lay curled in a ball, paralyzed and scarcely able to breathe.

That time her husband Mr. Frisby had been alive, and between them, taking turns, they had managed to carry Timothy to Mr. Ages' house. It was a sad and frightening journey, and when they arrived they had been afraid he might already be dead. Mr. Ages looked at him, examined his tongue, felt his pulse, and found a small red lump near his neck. "Spider," he said. "Not a black widow, but bad enough." He had forced a few drops of a milky liquid into Timothy's mouth and held him upright so that it could trickle down his throat, for Timothy could not swallow. In a few minutes his small muscles had unlocked, and he was able to move his arms and legs. "He'll be all right," said Mr. Ages, "but weak for a few hours."

The trip back home had been a happy one, and the other children were wide-eyed with joy to see Timothy alive. Yet Mrs. Frisby thought that this had been the beginning of his frailness. From that time on he tended to stumble a little when he walked, especially when he was tired; he never grew as big or as vigorous as his brother Martin. But he thought a great deal more, and in that he resembled his father.

Now she reached Mr. Ages' house, a hole in the brick wall where one end of heavy floor beam had once rested. It was about two feet below the top of the wall, and one reached it by climbing down a sort of rough stairway of broken brick ends. She knocked on his door, made of a piece of shingle. "Oh, let him be in, *please*," she thought, but he was not. There was no answer, so she sat down to wait on the narrow ledge of brick in front of his door.

Half an hour passed, the sun sinking lower in the west all the time, before she heard a slight scratching noise up above, and there he came, carrying a cloth sack bulging with some kind of lumpy material. His fur was a soft gray-white, and so glossy he seemed almost to glow. Mrs. Frisby had heard that Mr. Ages was not truly a white mouse; that is, he had not been born with white fur, but had turned white from old age. Whether this was so or not she did not know. Certainly he *seemed* very old, and very wise; yet he walked nimbly enough.

"Oh, Mr. Ages, I'm so glad you've come," she said. "I don't suppose you remember me, Mrs. Frisby."

"Of course I remember you. And I was sad to hear about poor Mr. Frisby. How is your young son—Timothy, was it?"

"It's about him I've come to see you. He's taken terribly sick."

"Has he? I was afraid he might turn out to be not as strong as the others."

"I hoped you might be able to help him."

"That may be. Come in, please, so I can put down this sack."

Mr. Ages' house, somewhat larger than a shoebox but about the same shape, resembled the house of a hermit. It was bare of furniture except for a bit of bedding in one corner, a stool made of a piece of brick, and another piece of brick worn smooth from use as a pestle on which he ground out his medicines. Along one entire wall, arranged neatly in small piles, stood the raw materials he had collected: roots, seeds, dried leaves, pods, strips of bark and shriveled mushrooms.

To this row he now added the contents of his sack. It held a number of small plants, all of them the same kind, with stringy roots and dark, veined green leaves that looked like mint.

"Pipsissewa," said Mr. Ages. "Botanically, *Chima-*

16

phila umbellata. It stays green all winter, and makes a very useful spring tonic. Most people use only the leaves, but I have found the roots even more effective." He arranged the plants in an orderly pile. "But that's not what you're here for. What's wrong with young Timothy?"

"He has a very high fever. He's delirious. I don't know what to do."

"How high?"

"So high that he feels burning hot to the touch, runs with perspiration, and yet he shivers with cold at the same time.

"Keep him wrapped up in a blanket."

"I do."

"And his pulse?"

"So fast that you cannot tell one heartbeat from the next."

"His tongue?"

"So coated that it looks purple."

"How does he breathe?"

"He breathes very rapidly, and the air rasps in his chest. He said, at first, that he could not get his breath."

"But he does not cough."

"No."

"He has pneumonia," said Mr. Ages. "I have some medicine that will help him. But the most important thing is to keep him warm. And he must stay in bed." He went to the back of his house, and from a ledge formed by a projecting brick he took three packets of medicine, powders neatly wrapped in white paper.

"Give him one of these tonight. Mix it in water and make him drink it. If he is still delirious, hold his nose

18

and pour it down his throat. Give him the second one tomorrow morning, and the third the next morning."

Mrs. Frisby took the packages. "Will he get better?" she asked, dreading to hear the answer.

"He will get better this time. His fever will be less on the second day, and gone the third, after he has taken all the medicine. That does not mean he will have recovered; his lungs will still be terribly weak and sensitive. If he gets the least bit cold, or breathes cold air—even a breath or two—the pneumonia will surely come back worse than before. And the second time he may not recover. This will be true for at least three weeks, and more likely a month."

"And after that?"

"Even after that he should be careful, though we may hope by then the weather will be warmer."

By now the sun was getting low in the west, settling into the high mountains beyond the woods. Mrs. Frisby thanked Mr. Ages and set out for home as quickly as she could go.

The Crow
and the Cat

Mrs. Frisby looked again at the sun and saw that she faced an unpleasant choice. She could go home by the same roundabout way she had come, in which case she would surely end up walking alone in the woods in the dark—a frightening prospect, for at night the forest was alive with danger. Then the owl came out to hunt, and foxes, weasels and strange wild cats stalked among the tree trunks.

The other choice would be dangerous, too, but with luck it would get her home before dark. That would be to take a straighter route, across the farmyard between the barn and the chicken house, going not too close to the house but cutting the distance home by half. The cat would be there somewhere, but by daylight— and by staying in the open, away from the shrubs— she could probably spot him before he saw her.

The cat: He was called Dragon. Farmer Fitzgibbon's wife had given him the name as a joke when he was a small kitten pretending to be fierce. But when he grew up, the name turned out to be an apt one. He was enormous, with a huge, broad head and a large mouth full of curving fangs, needle sharp. He had seven claws on each foot and a thick, furry tail, which lashed angrily from side to side. In color he was orange and white, with glaring yellow eyes; and when he leaped to kill, he gave a high, strangled scream that froze his victims where they stood.

But Mrs. Frisby preferred not to think about that. Instead, as she came out of the woods from Mr. Ages' house and reached the farmyard fence she thought about Timothy. She thought of how his eyes shone with merriment when he made up small jokes, which he did frequently, and how invariably kind he was to his small, scatterbrained sister Cynthia. The other children sometimes laughed at her when she made mistakes, or grew impatient with her because she was forever losing things; but Timothy never did. Instead, he would help her find them. And when Cynthia herself had been sick in bed with a cold, he had sat by her side for hours and entertained her with stories. He made these up out of his head, and he seemed to have a bottomless supply of them.

Taking a firm grip on her packets of medicine, Mrs. Frisby went under the fence and set out toward the farmyard. The first stretch was a long pasture; the barn itself, square and red and big, rose in the distance to her right; to her left, farther off, were the chicken houses.

When at length she came abreast of the barn, she saw the cattle wire fence that marked the other end of the pasture; and as she approached it, she was startled by a sudden outburst of noise. She thought at first it was a hen, strayed from the chickenyard—caught by a fox? She looked down the fence and saw that it was no hen at all, but a young crow, flapping in the grass, acting most odd. As she watched, he fluttered to the top wire of the fence, where he perched nervously for a moment. Then he spread his wings, flapped hard, and took off— but after flying four feet he stopped with a snap and crashed to the ground again, shedding a flurry of black feathers and squawking loudly.

He was tied to the fence. A piece of something silvery —it looked like wire—was tangled around one of his legs; the other end of it was caught in the fence. Mrs. Frisby walked closer, and then she could see it was not wire after all, but a length of silver-colored string, probably left over from a Christmas package.

The crow was sitting on the fence, pecking ineffectively at the string with his bill, cawing softly to himself, a miserable sound. After a moment he spread his wings, and she could see he was going to try to fly again.

"Wait," said Mrs. Frisby.

The crow looked down and saw her in the grass.

"Why should I wait? Can't you see I'm caught? I've got to get loose."

"But if you make so much noise again the cat is sure to hear. If he hasn't heard already."

"You'd make noise, too, if you were tied to a fence with a piece of string, and with night coming on."

"I would not," said Mrs. Frisby, "if I had any sense and knew there was a cat nearby. Who tied you?" She was trying to calm the crow, who was obviously terrified.

He looked embarrassed and stared at his feet. "I picked up the string. It got tangled with my foot. I sat on the fence to try to get it off, and it caught on the fence."

"*Why* did you pick up the string?"

The crow, who was very young indeed—in fact, only a year old—said wearily, "Because it was shiny."

"You knew better."

"I had been told."

Birdbrain, thought Mrs. Frisby, and then recalled what her husband used to say: The size of the brain is no measure of its capacity. And well she might recall it, for the crow's head was double the size of her own.

"Sit quietly," she said. "Look toward the house and see if you see the cat."

"I don't see him. But I can't see behind the bushes. Oh, if I could just fly higher . . ."

"Don't," said Mrs. Frisby. She looked at the sun; it was setting behind the trees. She thought of Timothy, and of the medicine she was carrying. Yet she knew she could not leave the foolish crow there to be killed—and killed he surely would be before sunrise—just for want of a few minutes' work. She might still make it by dusk if she hurried.

"Come down here," she said. "I'll get the string off."

"How?" said the crow dubiously.

"Don't argue. I have only a few minutes." She said this in a voice so authoritative that the crow fluttered down immediately.

"But if the cat comes . . ." he said.

"If the cat comes, he'll knock you off the fence with one jump and catch you with the next. Be still." She was already at work with her sharp teeth, gnawing at the string. It was twined and twisted and twined again around his right ankle, and she saw she would have to cut through it three times to get it off.

As she finished the second strand, the crow, who was staring toward the house, suddenly cried out:

"I see the cat!"

"*Quiet!*" whispered Mrs. Frisby. "Does he see us?"

"I don't know. Yes. He's looking at me. I don't think he can see you."

"Stand perfectly still. Don't get in a panic." She did not look up, but started on the third strand.

"He's moving this way."

"Fast or slow?"

"Medium. I think he's trying to figure out what I'm doing."

She cut through the last strand, gave a tug, and the string fell off.

"There, you're free. Fly off, and be quick."

"But what about you?"

"Maybe he hasn't seen me."

"But he will. He's coming closer."

Mrs. Frisby looked around. There was not a bit of cover anywhere near, not a rock nor a hole nor a log; nothing at all closer than the chicken yard—and that was in the direction the cat was coming from, and a long way off.

"Look," said the crow. "Climb on my back. Quick. And hang on."

Mrs. Frisby did what she was told, first grasping the precious packages of medicine tightly between her teeth.

"Are you on?"

"Yes."

She gripped the feathers on his back, felt the beat of his powerful black wings, felt a dizzying upward surge, and shut her eyes tight.

"Just in time," said the crow, and she heard the angry scream of the cat as he leaped at where they had just been. "It's lucky you're so light. I can scarcely tell

25

you're there." Lucky indeed, thought Mrs. Frisby; if it had not been for your foolishness, I'd never have gotten into such a scrape. However, she thought it wise not to say so, under the circumstances.

"Where do you live?" asked the crow.

"In the garden patch. Near the big stone."

"I'll drop you off there." He banked alarmingly, and for a moment Mrs. Frisby thought he meant it literally. But a few seconds later—so fast does the crow fly—they were gliding to earth a yard from her front door.

"Thank you very much," said Mrs. Frisby, hopping to the ground.

"It's I who should be thanking you," said the crow. "You saved my life."

"And you mine."

"Ah, but that's not quite even. Yours wouldn't have been risked if it had not been for me—me and my piece of string." And since this was just what she had been thinking, Mrs. Frisby did not argue.

"We all help one another against the cat," she said.

"True. Just the same, I am in debt to you. If the time ever comes when I can help you, I hope you will ask me. My name is Jeremy. Mention it to any crow you see in these woods, and he will find me."

"Thank you," said Mrs. Frisby. "I will remember."

Jeremy flew away to the woods, and she entered her house, taking the three doses of medicine with her.

Mr. Fitzgibbon's Plow

When Mrs. Frisby went into her house, she found Timothy asleep and the other children waiting, frightened, sad and subdued.

"He went to sleep right after you left," Teresa said. "He's waked up twice, and the second time he wasn't delirious. He said his chest hurt and his head hurt. But Mother, he seemed so weak—he could hardly talk. He asked where you were, and I told him. Then he went back to sleep."

Mr. Frisby went to where Timothy lay, a small ball of damp fur curled under a bit of cloth blanket. He looked scarcely larger then he had when she and Mr.

Frisby had carried him to Mr. Ages as an infant, and the thought of that trip made her wish Mr. Frisby were alive to reassure the children and tell them not to worry. But he was not, and it was she who must say it.

"Don't worry," she said. "Mr. Ages gave me some medicine for him and says he will recover." She mixed the contents of one of the packets, a gray-green powder, in water, and then gently shook Timothy awake.

He smiled. "You're back," he said in a voice as small as a whisper.

"I'm back, and I've brought you some medicine. Mr. Ages says it will make you all right." She lifted his head on her arm, and he swallowed the medicine. "I expect it's bitter," she said.

"It's not so bad," he said. "It tastes like pepper." And he fell back to sleep immediately.

The next morning, as predicted, his fever was lower, his breathing grew easier, and his heartbeat slowed down; still, that day he slept seven hours out of each eight. The next day he stayed awake longer, and on the third day he had no fever at all, just as Mr. Ages had said. However, since Mr. Ages had been right in all that, Mrs. Frisby knew he was sure to have been right in the other things he had said: Timothy was not really strong yet. He must stay in bed, stay warm, and breathe only warm air.

During those three days she had stayed close by his side, but on the fourth she felt cheerful enough to go for a walk, and also to fetch some more of the corn from the stump so they could have it for supper.

She went out her front door into the sunshine and was surprised to find a spring day waiting for her. The

28

weather had turned warm while she had stayed indoors; February was over and March had come in, as they say, like a lamb. There was a smell of dampness in the air as the frosted ground thawed, a smell of things getting ready to grow. It made her feel even more cheerful than before, and she walked almost gaily across the garden.

And yet despite the fine warmth of the day—indeed, in a way, because of it—Mrs. Frisby could not quite get rid of a nagging worry that kept flickering in her mind; it was the kind of worry that, if you push it out of this corner of your thoughts, pops up in that corner, and finally in the middle, where it has to be faced. It was the thought of Moving Day.

Everybody knows that the ground hog comes up from the deep hole where he has slept away the winter, looks around, and if he decides the cold weather is not over, goes back down to sleep for another six weeks. Field mice like Mrs. Frisby are not so lucky. When winter is over, they must move out of the garden and back to the meadow or the pasture. For as soon as the weather allows, Farmer Fitzgibbon's tractor comes rumbling through, pulling the sharp-bladed plow through the soil, turning over every foot of it. No animal caught in the garden that day is likely to escape alive, and all the winter homes, all the tunnels and holes and nests and cocoons, are torn up. After the plow comes the harrow, with its heavy creaking disks, and then the people with hoes and seeds.

Not all the field mice move into the garden for the winter, of course. Some find their way to barn lofts; some even creep into people's houses and live under the eaves or in attics, taking their chances with mousetraps.

29

But the Frisbys had always come to the garden, preferring the relative safety and freedom of the outdoors.

Moving Day therefore depends on the weather, and that is why a fine day set Mrs. Frisby worrying, even as she enjoyed it. As soon as the frost was out of the ground, the plow would come, and that could happen as much as a month earlier (or later) one year than the last.

And the worry was this: If it came too soon, Timothy would not be able to move. He was supposed to stay in bed, and moving meant a long walk across the field of winter wheat, up and down the hill to the brook's edge, where the Frisbys made their summer home. Not only that—the home itself would be damp and chilly for the first few weeks (as summer homes always are) until early spring turned to late spring and the nights grew truly warm. This was something that Mrs. Frisby and the children did not ordinarily mind; Moving Day, in fact, was normally a gay time, for it marked the end of the gray weather and the frost. It was like the beginning of a summer holiday.

But this year? Now that Mrs. Frisby had faced the problem, she did not see any answer except to hope that the day would not come too early. In another month (according to Mr. Ages), Timothy would be strong enough. Perhaps she was only borrowing trouble. One warm day, she told herself, does not make a summer. No, nor even a spring.

She walked on through the garden and saw ahead of her a small figure she knew. It was a lady shrew, a tiny thing scarcely bigger than a peanut, but with a wit as sharp as her teeth. She lived in a simple hole in the

ground a few yards away; Mrs. Frisby met her often and had grown to like her, though shrews are generally unpopular, having a reputation for short tempers and extremely large appetites.

"Good morning," said Mrs. Frisby.

"Ah, Mrs. Frisby. Good morning indeed. Too good is what I'm thinking." The shrew was holding a stalk of straw, which she now thrust into the earth. It went down easily for two inches or more before it bent in her hand. "Look at that. The top of the frost is gone already. Another few days like this, and it will be all gone. Then we will have the tractor in here again, breaking everything up."

"So soon? Do you really think so?" asked Mrs. Frisby, her worry returning in a rush, stronger than before.

"He plows when the frost is gone. Remember the spring of sixty-five? That year he plowed on the eleventh day of March, and on a Sunday at that. I moved down to the woods that night and nearly froze to death in a miserable hollow log. And that day came after a week of days just like this."

Mrs. Frisby did remember it; her family, too, had shivered through those chilly nights. For the fact was, the earlier Moving Day came, the colder the nights were likely to be.

"Oh, dear," she said. "I hope it doesn't happen this year. Poor Timothy's too sick to move."

"Sick is he? Take him to Mr. Ages."

"I've been myself. But he was too weak to get out of bed, and still is."

"I'm sorry to hear that. Then we must hope for another frost, or that the tractor will break down. I wish someone would drive a tractor through *his* house and see how he likes it." So muttering, the lady shrew moved off, and Mrs. Frisby continued across the garden. The remark was illogical, of course, for they both knew that without Mr. Fitzgibbon's plow there would be no garden to live in at all, and there was no way he could turn the earth without also turning up their houses.

Or was there? What the shrew had said was meant to be sympathetic, but it was not helpful. It meant, Mrs. Frisby realized, that she, too, could see no solution to the problem. But that did not mean that there was none. She remembered something her husband, Mr. Frisby, used to say: All doors are hard to unlock until you have the key. All right. She must try to find the key. But where? Whom to ask?

And then, as if to make things worse, she heard a sound that filled her with alarm. It came from across the fence in the farmyard, a loud, sputtering roar. It was Mr. Fitzgibbon starting his tractor.

Five Days

The sound of the tractor did not necessarily mean that Mr. Fitzgibbon was getting ready to plow. He used it for many other things—hauling hay and firewood, for instance, and mowing, and clearing snow in the winter. Mrs. Frisby reminded herself of all this as she hurried over to the corner post.

That was a very thick fence post at the corner of the garden nearest the farmhouse and the tractor shed. She had discovered long ago that it had, a few inches above the ground, a convenient knot hole with a hollow place behind it in which she could hide, when she had reason to, and watch what was going on in the yard. The cat, Dragon, also knew of its existence, so she had to look sharply when she came out.

She came up carefully behind the post, stared this way and that, and then darted around it and up into the hole. All clear.

Mr. Fitzgibbon had backed the tractor out of the big, cluttered shed where he kept it. Leaving the motor idling, he climbed down from the seat and called to the house. In a moment his older son Paul came out, closing the door carefully behind him. Paul, at fifteen, was a quiet, hardworking boy, rather clumsy in his movements but strong and careful about his chores. In a few seconds he was followed by his younger brother Billy, who at age twelve was noisier and had an annoying habit of skimming rocks across the grass at anything that moved. Mrs. Frisby did not much care for Billy.

"All right, boys," said Mr. Fitzgibbon, "let's haul it out and see about that linch pin."

"It was just about worn through last fall, I remember," Paul said. The boys disappeared into the shed, and Mr. Fitzgibbon remounted the tractor; he turned it around and backed it slowly toward the shed, so that the rear end was out of Mrs. Frisby's sight.

There was some clanking and clanging inside the shed while Mr. Fitzgibbon, looking over his shoulder, worked some levers on the side of the tractor.

"All set?"

He shifted gears and eased the tractor forward again. Hitched behind it, clear of the ground, was the plow.

Mrs. Frisby's heart sank. Surely he was not going to start *now?*

But as soon as he had the plow out in the sunlight, Mr. Fitzgibbon turned the tractor's engine off. It died with a sputter, and they all gathered around the plow-hitch.

"Sure enough," said Mr. Fitzgibbon. "She's just about ready to shear. Paul, I'm glad you remembered that. If I order it today, Henderson's will have a new one in three or four days."

"It took five days last time," Paul said.

"Five, then. That's just about right anyway. It's too wet to plow now, but five days like this ought to dry the ground out. Let's grease up while we've got it out. Billy, get the grease gun."

In her hiding place. Mrs. Frisby breathed a sigh of relief, and then began to worry again immediately. Five days, although a respite, was too short. Three weeks, Mr. Ages had said, would be the soonest Timothy could get out of bed, the soonest he could live through a chill night without getting pneumonia again. She sighed and felt like weeping. If only the summer house were as warm as the cinder block house. But it was not, and even if it were, he could not make the long journey. They might try to carry him—but what was the use of that? Only to have him get sick again after the first night there.

She might, she thought, go back to Mr. Ages and see if he had any ideas that would help. Was there some medicine that would make Timothy get strong sooner? She doubted it; surely, if he had such medicine he would have given it to her the first time. She was thinking about this when she climbed out through the knot hole and slithered to the ground below—not ten feet from the cat.

Dragon lay stretched out in the sunlight, but he was not asleep. His head was up and his yellow eyes were open, staring in her direction. She gasped in terror and whirled around the fence post to put it between her and him. Then, without pausing, she set out on a dash across the garden as fast as she could run, expecting at any instant to hear the cat's scream and feel his great claws on her back. She reached the shrew's hole and considered for a fraction of a second diving into it, but it was too small.

Then she glanced back over her shoulder and saw an amazing sight. The cat had not moved at all! He was lying exactly as before, except that now one of his eyes was closed. The other, however, was still looking straight at her, so she did not pause, but raced on.

Finally, when she was a safe distance away—two thirds across the garden and nearly home—she stopped and looked again more carefully. The cat still lay there and seemed to have gone to sleep. That was so odd— so unheard of—she could hardly believe it. Feeling quite safe, but puzzled, she looked for a vantage point from which she could see better. By rights, she should be dead, and though she had escaped by what seemed almost a miracle, she scolded herself for having been so care- less. If the cat had killed her, who would take care of the children?

She saw a dead asparagus plant, stiff, tall, with branches like a small tree. She climbed it and from near the top looked back to the farmyard. Mr. Fitzgibbon and his sons had finished greasing the tractor and gone on somewhere else. But the cat still lay on the grass, seemingly asleep. Why had he not chased her? Was it possible that, close as she had been, he had not seen her? She could not believe that. The only explanation she could think of was that he had just finished a very large meal and was feeling so stuffed and lazy he did not want to take the trouble to get up. But that was almost as unbelievable; certainly it had never happened before. Was it possible that he was sick?

Then, on what had already been a day of oddities and alarms, she noticed something else strange. Beyond the cat, quite far beyond, between the barn and the house, she saw what looked like a troop of dark gray figures marching in columns. Marching? Not exactly, but moving slowly and all in line.

They were rats.

There were a dozen of them, and at first she could not quite see what they were up to. Then she saw something moving, between them and behind them. It looked like a thick piece of rope, a long piece, maybe twenty feet. No. It was stiffer than rope. It was electric cable, the heavy, black kind used for outdoor wiring and strung on telephone poles. The rats were hauling it laboriously through the grass, inching it along in the direction of a very large wild rosebush in the far corner of the yard. Mrs. Frisby quickly guessed where they were taking it, though she could not guess why. In that rosebush, concealed and protected by dense tangles of fiercely sharp thorns, was the entrance to a rat hole. All the animals knew about it and were careful to stay away.

But what would the rats want with such a long piece of wire? Mrs. Frisby could not imagine. Even more curious, how did they dare to pull it across the yard in broad daylight when the cat was right there? The rats were bigger than Mrs. Frisby, and could be, when necessary, dangerous fighters, but they were no match for Dragon.

She watched them for quite a long time. It was obvious that they knew exactly what they were doing, and they looked as well drilled as a group of soldiers. They had about twenty-five yards to go to reach the rose-bush; as if at a signal (which, however, she was too far away to hear), they would all pull together, moving the wire about a foot. Then they would pause, rest, and heave again. It was about twenty minutes before the first rat disappeared into the bush. A little later the last bit of wire disappeared behind them like a thin black snake, and Mrs. Frisby climbed down from the asparagus bush.

All that time the cat had slept on.

A Favor
from Jeremy

In her worry about Moving Day, in watching the tractor, the cat, and finally the rats, Mrs. Frisby had forgotten that she had set out originally to get some corn for supper. Now she remembered it, so instead of continuing to her house she turned toward the far corner of the garden and the stump at the edge of the woods beyond. She was a little tired after her dash from the cat, so she walked along slowly, feeling the warmth of the sun and the smell of the breeze.

This mild breeze, carrying the moist essence of early spring, caused a dead leaf to flutter here and there, and across the garden near the fence it moved something that sparkled in the sunlight. This caught the corner of Mrs. Frisby's eye; she glanced at it, saw that it was only a bit of tin foil (or aluminum foil) blown from somewhere, and she looked away again. Then she looked back, for at that moment a black object plummeted from the sky, and she recognized her friend Jeremy the crow.

A thought crossed Mrs. Frisby's mind. She changed direction again, and, moving more quickly, ran across the earth to where Jeremy stood. He was hopping around the shiny piece of foil, eyeing it from one direction and another.

What had occurred to Mrs. Frisby was that although Jeremy was not the brightest of animals she had met, and though he was young, he knew things and places she did not, and one had to begin somewhere. As she approached him, he had picked up the foil in his beak and was spreading his wings to fly off.

"Wait, please," she called.

He turned, folded his wings, and then replaced the foil carefully on the ground.

"Hello," he said.

"You remember me?"

"Of course. You saved me from the cat." Then he added, "What do you think of this piece of foil?"

Mrs. Frisby looked at it without much interest.

"It's just a piece of foil," she said. "It's not very big."

"True. But it's shiny—especially when the sun strikes it just so."

"Why are you so interested in shiny things?"

"Well, really, I'm not. At least not very. But I have a friend who likes them, so when I see one I pick it up."

"I see. That's very thoughtful. And would the friend

be female?"

"As a matter of fact, yes. She is. How did you know?"

"Just a guess," said Mrs. Frisby. "Do you remember saying once that if I needed help, I might ask you?"

"I do. Any time. Just ask for Jeremy. Any of the crows can find me. And now, if you will excuse me . . ." He bent over to pick up the foil again.

"Please don't go yet," said Mrs. Frisby. "I think perhaps you can help me now."

"Ah," said Jeremy. "What kind of help? Are you hungry? I'll bring you some seeds from the barn loft. I know where they're stored."

"No, thank you," said Mrs. Frisby. "We have enough to eat." And then she told him, as briefly as she could, about Timothy, his sickness, and the problem of Moving Day. Jeremy knew about Moving Day; crows do not have to move, but they keep a close watch on such activities as plowing and planting so as to get their fair share of what's planted, and with their sharp eyes they see the small animals leaving before the plow.

So he clucked sympathetically when he heard Mrs. Frisby's story, cocked his head to one side, and thought as hard as he could for as long as he could, which was about thirty seconds. His eyes closed with the effort.

"I don't know what you should do," he said finally. "I'm sorry. But maybe I can help even so. At least, I can tell you what we do when we don't know what to do."

"We?"

"The crows. Most of the birds."

"What do you do, then?"

"Over that way," Jeremy nodded in the direction of the deep woods and faraway mountains that rose beyond the fence, "about a mile from here there grows a very large beech tree, the biggest tree in the whole forest. Near the top of the tree there is a hollow in the trunk. In the hollow lives an owl who is the oldest animal in the woods—some say in the world.

"When we don't know what to do, we ask him. Sometimes he answers our questions, sometimes he doesn't. It depends on how he feels. Or as my father used to say— what kind of a humor he's in."

Or possibly, thought Mrs. Frisby, on whether or not he knows the answer. But she said:

"Could you ask him, then, if he knows of any help for me?" She did not think it likely that he would.

"Ah, no," Jeremy said, "that won't do. That is, I could ask him, but I don't think the owl would listen. Imagine. A crow come to ask for help for a lady mouse with a sick child. He wouldn't believe me."

"Then what's to be done?"

"What's to be done? You must go yourself and ask him."

"But I could never find the tree. And if I did, I don't

think I could climb so high."

"Ah, now. That is where I can help, as I said I would. I will carry you there on my back, the way I did before. And home again, of course."

Mrs. Frisby hesitated. It was one thing to leap on a crow's back when the cat is only three jumps away and coming fast, but quite another to do it deliberately, and to fly deep into a dark and unknown forest. In short, Mrs. Frisby was afraid.

Then she thought of Timothy, and of the big steel plow blade. She told herself: I have no choice. If there is any chance that the owl might be able to help me, to advise me, I must go. She said to Jeremy:

"Thank you very much. I will go and talk to the owl if you will take me. It's a great favor."

"It's nothing," said Jeremy. "You're welcome. But we can't go now."

"Why not?"

"In the daytime, when the sun is out, the owl goes deep into the hollow and sleeps. That is, they say he sleeps, but I don't believe it. How could anyone sleep so long? I think he sits in there, part of the time at least, and thinks. And that's why he knows so much.

"But anyway, he won't speak in the daytime, not to anyone. And at night he's out flying, flying and hunting . . ."

"I know," said Mrs. Frisby—and that was another reason to be afraid.

"The time to see him is just at dusk. Then, when the light gets dim, he comes to the entrance of the hollow and watches while the dark comes in. That's the time to ask him questions."

43

"I understand," said Mrs. Frisby. "Shall we go this evening?"

"At five o'clock," Jeremy said, "I'll be at your house." He picked up the piece of foil in his bill, waved goodbye, and flew off.

The Owl

Jeremy appeared as promised when the last thumbnail of sun winked out over the mountains beyond the meadow. Mrs. Frisby was waiting, her heart pounding in her ears, and three of the children were there to watch—Teresa and Martin standing beside their mother, and Cynthia, who was afraid of the crow, just a pair of round eyes peering out the round doorway. Timothy was down below, taking a nap, and had not been told about the expedition lest he worry and blame himself for the risk his mother must take. (Indeed, the words Moving Day had not been mentioned in his presence.) Even to the other children Mrs. Frisby had explained

45

only a part of the problem; that is, she had not told them that there were only five days left, nor anything about Mr. Fitzgibbon and the tractor. She did not want them to worry, either.

Jeremy landed with a *swoosh*—a bit dramatically, perhaps—and nodded at the children and Mrs. Frisby.

"Hello," he said. "Here I am."

Mrs. Frisby introduced Martin and Teresa (and Cynthia's eyes). Martin, who wished he were going on the trip himself, asked Jeremy in excitement:

"How high can you fly?"

"Oh, I don't know exactly," Jeremy said. "A couple of miles, I guess."

"Mother, did you hear? You'll be two *miles* up in the air."

"Martin, it won't be necessary to go so high on this trip."

Jeremy said cheerfully: "No, but I can, if you'd like."

"No, thank you. I wouldn't think of your taking the trouble." She was trying hard to hide her terror, and Martin had not helped matters at all. But Jeremy suddenly saw that she was trembling and realized that she must be afraid.

"It's all right," he said kindly. "There's nothing to be nervous about. I fly over the woods a dozen times a day."

Yes, thought Mrs. Frisby, but *you're* not riding on your back, and *you* can't fall off.

"All right," she said as bravely as she could. "I'm ready. Teresa and Martin, take care of Timothy until I come back, and be sure you don't tell him where I've

46

gone." With a small leap she was on Jeremy's back, lying as flat as she could and holding tight to the glossy
feathers between his wings, as a horseback rider grips the
horse's mane before a jump. Martin and Teresa waved
goodbye, but she did not see them, for she had her face
pressed against the feathers and her eyes closed.

Once again she felt the surge of power as the crow's
broad wings beat down against the air; this time it lasted
longer for they were going higher than before. Then
the beating became gentler as they leveled off, and then,
to her alarm, it stopped altogether. What was wrong?
The crow must have felt her grow tense, for suddenly
from ahead she heard his voice:

"An updraft," he said. "We're soaring. There's usually one over this stretch of woods in the evening." A current of warm air, rising from the woods, was carrying them along. So smooth was the motion that they seemed to stand still, and Mrs. Frisby ventured to open her eyes and lift her head just a trifle. She could not look straight down—that was Jeremy's back—but off to the right, and a bit behind them, she saw a gray-brown square the size of a postage stamp. She realized with a gasp that it was the garden patch, and Martin and Teresa, if they were still there, were too small to be seen.

"Look to the left," said Jeremy, who was watching her over his shoulder. She did, and saw what looked like a wide, fearsome snake, blue-green in color, coiling through the woods.

"What is it?" she asked in wonder.

"You really don't know? It's the river."

"Oh," said Mrs. Frisby, rather ashamed of her ignorance. She had heard of the river, of course, but had not known that it looked like a snake. She had never been there, since to reach it one had to cross the entire width of the forest. There were advantages to being a bird.

In a minute more they had left the updraft, and Jeremy's wings resumed pumping. They went higher, and Mrs. Frisby closed her eyes again. When she opened them, the garden patch had vanished far behind them, and Jeremy, searching the trees below, began a long, slanting descent. Eventually, as he banked sharply, Mrs. Frisby saw off his wing tip a gray-brown patch among a stand of tall green pines; from so high it looked like a gnarled gray bush, but as they circled lower she could see that it was in fact an enormous tree, leafless, skeletal, and partly dead. One huge branch had recently broken off and fallen, and three pine trunks lay bent double under its weight. It was a gloomy and primeval spot, deeply shadowed in the gray dusk. Jeremy circled over it one more time, looking at a certain mark three-fourths of the way up the towering main trunk. Just below this spot another great branch, itself as big as an ordinary tree, jutted out over the tops of the pines, and on this at last Jeremy fluttered gently to rest. They were some ten feet from the main trunk, and Mrs. Frisby could see, just above the place where the branch joined the tree, a dark round hole as large as a lunch plate.

"We're here," Jeremy said in a low voice. "There's where he lives."

"Should I get down?" Instinctively, Mrs. Frisby spoke in a whisper.

"Yes. We've got to walk closer. But quietly. He doesn't like loud noises."

"It's so high." She still clung to the crow's back.

"But the limb is broad. You'll be safe enough."

And indeed the limb was almost as wide as a sidewalk. Mrs. Frisby gathered her courage, slithered down, and felt the solid wood under her feet; still she could not help thinking about how far it was to the ground below.

"There he is," said Jeremy, staring at the hole. "It's just the right time."

They inched their way along the limb, Mrs. Frisby gripping the rough bark tightly, being careful not to stumble; and as they came closer, she could dimly perceive a shape like a squat vase sitting back in the hollow of the tree. Near the top of the vase, wide apart, two round yellow eyes glowed in the dark.

49

"He can't see us," Jeremy whispered. "It's still too light."

Perhaps not, but he could hear, for now a deep round voice, a voice like an organ tone, echoed out of the hollow trunk:

"Who is standing outside my house?"

Jeremy answered:

"Sir, I am a crow. My name is Jeremy. And I have brought a friend. I hope we have not disturbed you. My friend needs your advice."

"I see. And can your friend not speak for himself?"

"Sir, my friend is a lady, a lady mouse."

"A mouse?" The sonorous voice sounded unbelieving. "Why should a crow be a friend to a mouse?"

"I was trapped, sir, and she set me free. She saved me from the cat."

"That is possible," said the owl, "though unusual. I have heard of such a thing before. We all help one another against the cat."

"True. And now, sir, my friend herself is in trouble."

"I understand," said the owl, moving closer to the round entrance of his hollow. "Mrs. Mouse, I cannot see you, for the glare of the daylight is too bright. But if you will step inside my house, I will listen to what you have to say."

Mrs. Frisby hesitated. She knew something of the dietary habits of owls, and she did not much like the idea of being trapped in his house. Finally she said timidly:

"Sir, I would not want to intrude. And I can hear you quite well from out here."

"Mrs. Mouse, please understand that I have no interest

at all, as a general rule, in helping mice to solve their problems. If you have indeed saved a bird from the cat, I will spare you a few minutes. But I do not discuss problems with people I cannot see. Either come inside, or tell your friend to take you home again."

Behind her, Mrs. Frisby heard Jeremy whisper, very softly, "It's all right. He wouldn't harm you in his own home."

She whispered back, "I hope not." She walked up the limb to the hollow, climbed over the sill and stepped inside.

Up so close, the owl looked very large. Each of his feathery feet was tipped with five gleaming talons an inch long. His beak was curved and sharp and cruel. He blinked his yellow eyes and said:

"Please step across the room, away from the light."

Mrs. Frisby did as she was told. As she grew accustomed to the dimness, she looked around her. The chamber into which she had stepped was spacious—at that level, almost half of the huge trunk was hollow—and clean, but the floor was extremely rough. It was not really a floor at all, but only the jagged ends of dead wood sticking up from below, like stalagmites in a cave, so that Mrs. Frisby had to climb rather than walk as she crossed the room. In the back the walls narrowed to a corner, and there she saw that the owl had built himself a nest, as big as a water bucket, of twigs and leaves; from the top she could see protruding some wisps of the feathers with which he had lined it.

When she got near this nest, she stopped and faced the owl, who had turned from the light of the doorway and was peering at her with his great yellow eyes. Jeremy was nowhere to be seen. She could only hope he was still waiting on the limb outside.

"Now," said the owl, "you may state your problem."

"Go to the Rats"

Mrs. Frisby began nervously, trying to arrange her thoughts:

"It's about my youngest son, Timothy. He is sick, too sick to leave his bed. And Moving Day is only five days off."

"Wait," said the owl. "Moving from where? Moving to where?"

"From the garden patch, where we're living, to the edge of the pasture by the stream."

"Which garden?" It had not occurred to Mrs. Frisby until now that a bird, flying freely over miles of countryside, would look down on many gardens.

"It belongs to Mr. Fitzgibbon."

"The one with the large stone?"

"Yes. My house is near the stone."

"What makes you so sure Moving Day will come in five days?"

Mrs. Frisby told him about the tractor, and what Mr. Fitzgibbon had said: five days until plowing. "Of course," she added, "it might turn cold again, and freeze, or even snow . . ."

"No," said the owl, sounding quite sure, "it will not. The wild onions are already up in the pastures." He asked her then what kind of house she had, and exactly where it was in relation to the big stone; apparently he knew the spot well.

But the more she talked to him, the more Mrs. Frisby became convinced that he would produce no solution to her problem. It had been foolish of her to think he could, foolish of her to come at all. Because, she thought, there really *was* no solution. At last she fell silent, and the owl asked no more questions. Finally he said:

"Lying where it does, your house will inevitably be turned up by the plow, and probably broken to bits in the process. There is no feasible way to prevent this. My only advice to you is this: If you stay in the house you will surely be crushed and killed, all of you. Therefore, it is better to take your chances with moving. Wrap your son Timothy up as warmly as you can, help him as much as possible on the journey, and hope for warm weather on Moving Day. That way you are at least sure to save yourself and the other children."

The owl paused, turned away from her and looked again at the entrance to his hollow; the patch of light it admitted was growing steadily dimmer.

"And now, if you will excuse me—the night is falling, and I have no more time to spare. I regret that I can not give you a more satisfactory solution to your problem. Good evening, Mrs. . . ." he paused. "I don't believe you told me your name."

"Mrs. Frisby." The poor mouse spoke with a sob in her throat, for the owl had said exactly what she feared he would say. And she had no real hope for Timothy. The owl had said, in effect: Either Timothy alone must die, or they must all die together. Even if Moving Day should be extraordinarily warm, the nights were sure to be frosty, and that would be the end of him. Still, one must be polite, and she added sadly, "I thank you, sir, for listening to me. . . ."

But at the mention of her name an extraordinary change had come over the owl. He turned back to face her again and stared at her most intently. Indeed, he gave an agitated flutter of his wings and half flew, half hopped closer to her, bending forward until his great sharp beak was only a few inches from her face. Mrs. Frisby shrank back in fear. What had she done wrong?

"Did you say Mrs. Frisby?"

"Yes. You asked my name."

"Related to Jonathan Frisby?"

"Yes. He was my husband. He died last summer. He was Timothy's father. But how did you know about him?"

"That is not important," said the owl, drawing back a little and looking at her in a new way—almost as if with deference. "I will say this: His name was not unknown in these woods. And if you are his widow, that puts matters in a different light."

Something in the way he said this caused Mrs. Frisby's hopes to lift a little.

"What do you mean?" she asked.

"I mean, madame, that there *is* a way that your son's life might just possibly be saved. I did not mention it to you because I saw no way you could conceivably do it, and I did not want to arouse false hope. But if you are Jonathan Frisby's widow—then perhaps it can be done."

"I don't understand at all," said Mrs. Frisby. "What is this thing?"

"It is not a thing that I can do myself. You must go to the rats."

"To the rats? But I don't know any rats. They have nothing to do with me."

"I don't doubt that. They have little to do with anyone except themselves, and will have less as time goes on. Nonetheless, I think they will help you, and if they will, they can."

"But what can they do?"

"They must move your house to a place where it will be safe from the plow."

Now Mrs. Frisby's spirits fell again, and she said, almost bitterly:

"You are joking, sir; you are not serious. No rat could move my house. It is far too heavy, much too big."

"The rats on Mr. Fitzgibbon's farm have—things— ways—you know nothing about. They are not like the rest of us. They are not, I think, even like most other rats. They work at night, in secret. Mrs. Frisby, do you know their main entrance?"

"In the rosebush? Yes."

"Go there. You will find a sentry guarding the door. His name is Justin. Tell him who you are, and that you come at my request. Tell him that you want to see a rat named Nicodemus. I think they will let you in, though they may insist on swearing you to secrecy. If they should ask that, you must of course use your own judgement; but my advice would be to do as they ask."

Mrs. Frisby was close to complete bewilderment.

"Secrecy," she said. "Secrecy about what?"

"That I cannot reveal. I, too, have agreed to it. Also, there is much I do not know, though I have given advice on certain aspects of their—projects."

"Well," said Mrs. Frisby, "I don't understand at all. But if it might save Timothy, I will try to do what you say."

"Tell them," added the owl, "that I suggest moving the house into the lee of the stone. Remember that—the lee of the stone. Also, do not forget the names: Justin and Nicodemus."

"Justin. Nicodemus. The lee of the stone," repeated Mrs. Frisby. "I will remember." She was now so entirely puzzled that she did not think to ask what the phrase meant. Presumably the rats would know.

"And, Mrs. Frisby," said the owl, moving again toward the entrance to the hollow, "please understand: I was an admirer of your late husband, though I never met him in person. I wish you well. I hope your son's life can be saved. You see, I can understand your particular need, for I face a similar problem."

"You?" said Mrs. Frisby. "But you have no Moving Day."

"I have lived in this tree, in this same hollow," the owl said, "for more years then anyone can remember. But now, when the wind blows hard in winter and rocks the forest, I sit here in the dark, and from deep down in the bole, down near the roots, I hear a new sound. It is the sound of strands of wood creaking in the cold and snapping one by one. The limbs are falling; the tree is old, and it is dying. Yet I cannot bring myself, after so many years, to leave, to find a new home and move into it, perhaps to fight for it. I, too, have grown old. One of these days, one of these years, the tree will fall, and when it does, if I am still alive, I will fall with it."

With this sad prediction the owl stepped through his doorway, spread his great wings and was gone, soaring silently downward into the shadowy woods below.

Mrs. Frisby followed him out onto the limb. To her relief, Jeremy was still waiting where she had left him, though not very patiently.

"We must hurry," he said. "It's almost dark. I'm not supposed to be out so late." Mrs. Frisby, who had the same feeling, climbed on his back, much less afraid now for two reasons: First, she was getting used to air travel; second, since the woods below them were dark, she could no longer see how far away the ground was.

"He talked to you for a long time," said Jeremy as they flew. "Did he tell you anything that will help?"

"I don't know," said Mrs. Frisby. Since the owl had brought up the matter of secrecy, and had, in fact, been secretive himself, she was not sure just how much she should tell Jeremy.

"Why don't you know?"

"I mean, he told me some things, but I don't know whether they'll help or not." She decided to counter with a question of her own. "What does 'in the lee' mean?"

Jeremy, being like all birds knowledgeable about the wind, knew the answer to that. "It means the calm side, the side the wind doesn't blow from. When there's a strong wind, you fly up to the barn from the lee, so you don't get bashed into the wall. My father taught me that."

"I see," said Mrs. Frisby, and she became more puzzled than ever. What had the wind to do with it?

"He told me," she said finally, deciding it could do no harm, "to go and see the rats."

"The rats?" Jeremy was startled. "But they don't have anything to do with us."

"I know. But he thought they might help."

"What could they do?"

"He thought they might move my whole house. But how they could do it, I can't imagine."

"Oh, I don't doubt that they *could*," said Jeremy. "Everyone knows—at least all the birds know—that the rats can do things. They're up to something; nobody is quite sure what. For one thing, they're building themselves a new house, way back in the woods, over the mountains. They've even made quite a big clearing near it. I'd show you, but it's too dark now.

"They used to carry food, like the rest of us. But now we see them with other things—pieces of metal, and bits of machinery, and things I can't even recognize. They take them into that rosebush, and what happens to them I don't know. But the owl knows more than most. I expect he's had some dealings with them. Just the same, I've never heard of their helping anybody but themselves."

"Neither have I. But I'm going to ask them anyway. There isn't anyone else to ask."

By the time they reached the garden, it had gone almost completely dark, and Jeremy could not linger.

"Good night, Jeremy," said Mrs. Frisby, feeling almost affectionate toward the crow. "Thank you for taking me, and for waiting to bring me back."

"You're welcome," said Jeremy. "If you need me again, just ask. After all, if it weren't for you, I wouldn't be here to ask." And he flew off into the darkness, the last crow to get home that night.

In the Rosebush

When Mrs. Frisby got home, Teresa, Martin and Cynthia were eating supper, as she had told them to do if it got dark before she returned. Coming silently down the tunnel, she could hear them talking in the room below, and she paused a moment to eavesdrop on their conversation. Obviously Cynthia had been worrying, and Teresa was reassuring her.

"She couldn't have got back sooner than this, Cynnie. Don't you remember? The crow said it was a *mile* to the tree. It might even be farther."

"Yes, but crows fly so fast."

"But if he went two miles high"—that was Martin—

61

"it would be three miles altogether."

"Six," said Teresa. "Two up, two down, and one to get there and one to get back."

"That's right. No wonder she isn't back yet."

"But what about the owl? You know how owls are."

"It was still light when they got there. He couldn't see."

"But it's dark now," said Cynthia. "Oh, I *wish* she'd come back. I'm scared."

"Not so loud," Teresa said. "Timothy will hear."

"I'm home," called Mrs. Frisby, hurrying the rest of the way down.

And now it appeared that they had all been worried, for they ran to her, and even Martin, who ordinarily avoided such displays, threw his arms around her.

"Oh, Mother," cried Cynthia, near tears. "I was so worried."

"Poor Cynthia. It's all right."

"How high did you fly?" asked Martin, recovering quickly.

"High enough so the trees looked like bushes, the garden like a postcard, and the river like a snake."

"Did you see the owl? What did he say?"

"I saw him. Later, I'll tell you about it. First I want to see Timothy. How is he? Why didn't you move his bed out here?"

Teresa said: "I wanted to, but he said he'd rather stay in the bedroom. I think he's feeling worse again."

But when Mrs. Frisby went to see him, she found him sitting up, and his forehead felt not at all feverish.

"I'm all right," he said. "I stayed in here because I wanted to think about something."

62

"Think about what?"

"About Moving Day."

"Moving Day! But why? What about it?"

Had he, after all, overheard her talking to the others? Heard about her flight to the owl? But no, he was explaining.

"I haven't been outdoors since I got sick, so I don't know what it's like. I mean the weather. But today, this afternoon, I noticed something."

"What was that?"

"A smell in the air, a warm, wet smell. If you sniff you can still smell it, though it's not so strong now."

Mrs. Frisby had noticed this, of course, both indoors and out.

"It's the smell of the frost melting," Timothy went on. "I remember it from last year. And after that, it wasn't long until we moved. Mother, when are we going to move this year?"

"Oh, not for a long time yet." Mrs. Frisby tried to sound as casual as she could. "It's still much too cold, too early to think about it."

"I have to think about it," said Timothy. He sounded serious, but calm and unworried. "Because if it comes too soon, I don't know if I can go. I tried walking a little bit today, in here, when the others were outside."

"Timothy, you're supposed to stay in bed! You'll make yourself sick again."

"I know, I know. But I had to find out. And I didn't walk much. I couldn't. I only went a few steps, and I got so dizzy I had to lie down again."

"Of course you did. You haven't really recovered yet."

"I guess I haven't. That's why I wanted to think."

"Timothy, you *must* not worry about it. That will only make you worse."

"I'm not worried at all. I thought I would be, but I'm not—or maybe I think I should be, but I can't. What I really think about is how nice it is there, in the summer beside the brook, and it's true, I want to go. But I'm not scared. I was afraid you might be, or that you might think I was. That's really what I wanted to tell you. I'm just going to wait and see what happens. So you shouldn't worry about it, either."

Mrs. Frisby realized that he had somehow switched their positions. He had seen the danger he was in—guessed, somehow, that Moving Day was near, and that he was very likely to die. And yet here he was—reassuring her. She wanted to tell him about the owl and the rats, tell him that something still might be done. But she decided she had better not; she did not really know if they would help. It would be better to wait until she had seen them.

So instead she said, rather lamely: "Timothy, don't think about it any more. When the time comes, we'll see how you are and then decide what to do."

The next morning at daybreak she went to see the rats. She had never been in the rosebush before, never even really close to it, and now, the nearer she got, the more nervous she became. No one had ever told her—nor, as far as she knew, told any of the other animals—to keep away from it. It was just something one knew. The rats on Mr. Fitzgibbon's farm kept to themselves. One did not prowl in their domain.

64

She had, before coming out of the garden, looked around carefully to be sure Dragon was nowhere in sight. But even Dragon, though he would chase a rat up to the edge of the bush, would not follow him into it.

The thorns, of course, helped to discourage trespassers. Mrs. Frisby had never realized until that moment, standing next to it, how very big the bush was, how dense, how incredibly thorny. It was bigger than the tractor shed, and its branches were so densely intertwined that as small as she was, Mrs. Frisby could find no easy way to crawl into it, though she walked all the way around it looking. She remembered approximately where she had seen the rats go in, and she studied that part of the bush carefully. How had they done it?

Then she saw that on one branch, close to the ground, the thorns had been scraped off, and about a half-inch of it—just big enough for a handhold—was worn smooth. She put her hand on this and pushed timidly. The branch yielded easily, rather like a swinging door, and behind it she saw a trail, a sort of tunnel through the bush, wide enough so that she could walk into it without touching thorns on either side. When she went forward, she released the branch, and it swung back silently into place behind her. She was inside the bush, and it was dark.

She walked forward, peering into the dimness and following the small trail which wound in a curving course toward the center of the bush, its earthern floor packed firm by the pressure of small feet. Then, straight ahead of her, she saw the entrance.

She had expected—what? A round hole in the dirt, most likely, but certainly nothing like what she saw.

First, a sizeable clearing—about five feet across—had been cut from the center of the bush. Branches overhead had been cleared away, too, not quite to the top of the bush but almost, so that the sunlight filtered through easily, and soft moss grew on the ground. In the middle of this bright green cave rose a small mound, eight inches tall, in the end of which was an arched entrance neatly lined with stone, like a small doorway without any door. Behind the entrance a tunnel, its floor also lined with stones, led backward and downward.

Beside the entranceway, looking at her with dark, unblinking eyes, stood the biggest rat she had ever seen.

Brutus

S top where you are," said the rat. "How did you get
in here?"

"I walked in," said Mrs. Frisby, keeping her voice
calm with an effort. "I found a branch with the thorns
smoothed off. I pushed it back, and found . . ."

"I know," said the rat, rather rudely. "And now, walk
out again. You aren't allowed in here." He moved a few
inches toward her, placing himself between her and the
entrance. She noticed how powerful his muscles looked
under his glossy coat. He would almost be a match for
Dragon—almost, but not quite.

"Go on," he repeated.

68

"But I have a reason . . ."

"I don't care what you have. Go away. You're small. I wouldn't want to hurt you."

"Are you Justin?" Mrs. Frisby inched back as the rat inched forward.

"I'm Brutus. Justin's not here." That was reasonably obvious, Mrs. Frisby thought. The rat named Brutus added: "You know Justin?"

"No," said Mrs. Frisby. "That is, not exactly."

"If you don't know him, how do you know his name?" Brutus sounded puzzled, and Mrs. Frisby observed that although he was greatly oversized and muscular, and his eyes were bright enough, he looked very young.

"It was told to me by a friend. Can I see him?"

"Justin? No. He's at a meeting. I'm taking his place. They're all at a meeting but me."

Bad luck, thought Mrs. Frisby. He's a substitute. She said:

"Then I'll wait for him."

"No," said Brutus. "You can't stay here. I've got orders. Now go, or I'll have to take you out myself." He moved forward again.

"My name," said the mouse desperately, "is Mrs. Jonathan Frisby. I want to see Nicodemus." It did not work.

"I don't care what your name is, and you can't see Nicodemus, that's sure." Brutus now looked both puzzled and annoyed. "Move on, and be quick."

"All right," said Mrs. Frisby. "You needn't force me. I'll go." She turned slowly and walked back the way she had come. She felt like crying—after coming all this way, after flying to see the owl, to be turned back so abruptly at the end. She thought, as she walked into the darker part of the bush, maybe she could just wait for an hour or so, until the meeting (what kind of a meeting could it be?) was over and then go back, and perhaps the rat named Justin would be at the entrance then. But would Justin pay any more attention to her than Brutus had done? She had a feeling that he would.

But when she stopped she heard footsteps behind her. She looked back and saw that Brutus was following her, so she started again, hurrying to keep out of his sight. After a while she paused again and listened. This time there was no sound. He must have gone back to his post. She sat down on the ground.

Then, ahead of her, in the direction of the place where she had entered the bush, she heard a rustle, a faint scraping noise. It was the branch she had pushed to get in. Someone else was moving it. Someone was coming in, walking along the narrow path toward her. It must be another rat. Suddenly she was terrified. What would he do, meeting her unexpectedly in this dimness?

She shrank to one side, as close as she could get to the wall of thorns, hoping that whoever it was might go on past, not seeing her.

Then he came around the curve, and she saw him. It was her old friend, Mr. Ages, the white mouse.

He was moving extremely slowly, and she realized that he was limping badly. One of his legs was injured; it was wrapped up in splints and bandaged.

"Mr. Ages," she called softly, "it's Mrs. Frisby."

"Who?" He peered into the shadow. "I can't see you."

"Mrs. Frisby." She moved into the middle of the path in front of him.

"Why, so it is. Mrs. Frisby. How do you do?" He sounded cordial enough, but he was startled. "I didn't know that you . . . How do you happen to be in here?"

"It's a long story."

"Then tell it to me while I rest. I'm supposed to be at a meeting, but I'm late already, and a few minutes more won't matter. As you can see, I had a bad fall and broke my ankle."

"I'm sorry to hear that. I hope it doesn't hurt."

"It is mending. But I can walk only slowly and need to rest frequently." He sat down with a sigh. "Now tell me what you're doing in the rats' bush."

Mrs. Frisby (who was wondering the same thing about him) told him as briefly as she could about Timothy, Jeremy, the owl, and Brutus. Mr. Ages listened in silence, interrupting only once.

"You went *into* the owl's tree?"

"Yes. But I was afraid."

"I should think so. That took courage."

"I had to do it."

When she had finished her story, Mr. Ages sat quietly for a minute, considering it.

"Poor Timothy," he said at last. "I should have

thought of that myself. But, of course, when I gave you the medicine, the weather had not yet turned warm. Then I fell and broke my leg, and I forgot all about it." He stood up.

"I think," he said, "that you should come with me back to the entrance."

"But I can't. Brutus will still be there."

"Mrs. Frisby, having done all that you have done, you are not going to give up now. I'll talk to Brutus."

"You know him?"

"I have known him since he was born. He's not very old, you know. I think he will do what I ask." From the way he said this, Mrs. Frisby could tell he did not merely think it, he knew it. But how?

"All right," she said doubtfully. "I'll try again. But I don't understand. How do you know Brutus?"

"We had better move along." They started back toward the entrance at Mr. Ages' slow, limping pace. "As to how I know Brutus—that's a much longer story than yours, and I doubt that I'm the one to tell it to you. It is for Nicodemus to say.

"But I will tell you this: If we go in the entrance—as we will, if you are to ask for help—you must promise that you will never tell anyone anything at all about what you see and hear."

"I will promise," said Mrs. Frisby. Again, she thought, she had no choice. "The owl told me that, too."

When they approached the entrance again, Mrs. Frisby saw that Brutus stood at his post as before, but that another rat had joined him. Two of them, she thought. I hope Mr. Ages knows them both. The new rat saw them coming. He looked alert, dark gray in color, and extraordinarily handsome, though not so huge as Brutus.

"Mr. Ages," he said. "How's the leg?"

"Better. But it will be a while before I can run again."

"Justin," said Brutus, staring at Mrs. Frisby. "There she is. That's the one I was telling you about."

"Is she now." Justin looked at her casually. He did not sound particularly alarmed.

"Mrs. Frisby," said Mr. Ages formally, "may I present my friends Justin and Brutus?"

"How do you do?" Brutus sounded doubtful.

"Mrs. Frisby?" said Justin. "Not Mrs. Jonathan Frisby?"

"She is Mrs. Jonathan Frisby," said Mr. Ages. "A widow, as you know."

"Madame," said Justin, bowing politely, "it is an honor to meet you."

Brutus now looked astonished. "You both know her? Who is she?"

"Brutus," said Mr. Ages gently, "don't you remember Mr. Jonathan?"

Brutus wrinkled his brow. "Mr. Jonathan? You mean the one Dragon . . ."

"Yes," said Justin quickly. "And this is Mrs. Jonathan."

"Oh," said Brutus. Then, to Mrs. Frisby: "Why didn't you *tell* me. I wouldn't have chased you off."

"Well," said Mrs. Frisby, "I did try. But it doesn't matter."

"No," Mr. Ages added. "Because on the way out she met me coming in. She needs to talk to Nicodemus— and quickly."

Brutus looked doubtful again. "Nicodemus? But can

she? I mean, how about the rules? What about the Plan?"

Mr. Ages said: "That has been taken care of. She has promised secrecy, and she is to be trusted completely. That I, myself, guarantee. After all, consider who she is." As an afterthought he added, ". . . and who her children are."

Who am I, then? Mrs. Frisby asked herself in wonder. I suppose that, too, will have to come from Nicodemus.

Mr. Ages said to Justin: "What about the meeting? It can't be over already."

"It was temporarily adjourned," said Justin, "to wait for you. In fact, I came to find you."

"Then I suppose we had better go in."

Justin led the way through the arched entrance, with Mrs. Frisby and Mr. Ages following. Brutus remained outside at his post.

In the Library

The tunnel led gently downward, and after the first dozen steps they were in darkness. Mrs. Frisby could see nothing at all. Behind her Mr. Ages limped along; ahead she could hear the scuffle of Justin's footsteps. She followed the sound blindly. Then she heard his voice.

"Just walk straight forward, Mrs. Frisby. There's nothing to trip over, and nothing to bump into. If you get off course, you'll feel the wall." He added: "The dark part doesn't last long."

Now what did he mean by that? She thought it over for a minute or two as she walked and had just decided to ask him, when to her surprise she saw ahead of her a faint glow. A light! But how could there be a light down so far? "There, we're through it," said Justin cheerfully. "I know that blackout bit must be annoying the first time, but it's necessary."

"But aren't we under the ground?"

"Oh yes. About three feet down by now, I'd guess."

"Then how can it be light?"

"I could tell you," Justin said, "but if you'll wait fifteen seconds, you'll see for yourself."

In a few more steps the tunnel—Mrs. Frisby could now discern, dimly, its shape and direction—took a turn to the right, and she did see for herself. She stopped in astonishment.

Ahead of her stretched a long, well-lit hallway. Its ceiling and walls were a smoothly curved arch, its floor hard and flat, with a soft layer of carpet down the middle. The light came from the walls, where every foot or so on both sides a tiny light bulb had been recessed and the hole in which it stood, like a small window, had been covered with a square of colored glass—blue, green or yellow. The effect was that of stained-glass windows in sunlight.

Justin was watching her and smiling. "Do you like it? The carpet and the colored glass we don't really need. Some of the wives did that on their own, just for looks. They cut the glass, believe it or not, from old bottles. The carpet was a piece of trim they found somewhere."

"It's beautiful," Mrs. Frisby said. "But how . . ."

"We've had electricity for four years now."

"Five," said Mr. Ages.

"Five," said Justin agreeably. "The lights"—they were

the very small, very bright twinkling kind—"we found on trees. In fact, most of our lights come from trees. Not until after Christmas, of course—about New Year's. The big light bulbs we have trouble handling."

Mrs. Frisby was familiar with electricity (her husband, who knew all kinds of things, had once explained it to her). At night she had seen the lamps shining in Mr. Fitzgibbon's house, and at Christmas time the lights that his sons strung on a pine tree outside.

"You mean you just took them?" she asked.

"We were careful to take only a few from each tree," said Mr. Ages.

"It was like picking fruit," Justin said rather dreamily. "The annual light bulb harvest. We had to go quite far up the road before we had enough. Even so, it took two Christmases."

"Justin," said Mr. Ages, "I think we'd better get on."

They continued along the corridor, which curved always slightly to the right, so Mrs. Frisby could never really tell how long it was, and which soon began to incline more steeply into the ground. Mrs. Frisby noticed that the air, which should have been dank and damp so deep underground, was on the contrary fresh and clean, and she thought she could even detect a very faint breeze blowing past her ears as she moved.

In a few more minutes the hall widened abruptly into a large oval chamber. Here the lights were set in the ceiling; at the far end, Mrs. Frisby could see, the long tunnel continued and looked as if it slanted upward again—perhaps to another entrance, a back door. Was this, then, their destination, the main hall of the rats? But if so, where were all the other rats? The room was entirely empty—not even a stick of furniture.

"A storeroom," said Justin. "Sometimes full. Now empty."

Then she saw that off one side of the chamber there was a stairway leading down, and beside it a small door. Justin led them to the door.

"For freight only," he said with a grin at Mr. Ages. "But considering your limp, I think we can make an exception. The stairs wouldn't be easy."

Mrs. Frisby looked at the stairway. It went down in a spiral and each step was neatly inlaid with a rectangular piece of slate. She could not tell how far down it led, since after the first turn of the spiral she could see no more, but she had a feeling it was a long way down. As Justin said, it would be hard for Mr. Ages.

Justin opened the door. It led into a square room that looked like a closet.

"After you," he said. Mrs. Frisby went in, the others followed, and the door swung shut. On the wall were two knobs. Justin pushed one of them, and Mrs. Frisby, who had never been in an elevator before, gasped and almost fell as she felt the floor suddenly sink beneath her feet. Justin reached out a hand to steady her.

"It's all right," he said. "I should have warned you."

"But we're falling!"

"Not quite. We're going down, but we've got two strong cables and an electric motor holding us."

Still, Mrs. Frisby held her breath during the rest of the descent, until finally the small elevator came to a gentle stop and Justin opened the door. Then she breathed again and looked out.

The room before her was at least three times as big as the one they had just left, and corridors radiated from it in as many directions as petals from a daisy. Directly opposite the elevator an open arch led into what looked like a still larger room—seemingly some kind of an assembly hall, for it had a raised platform at one end.

And now there were rats. Rats by dozens—rats standing and talking in groups of twos and threes and fours, rats walking slowly, rats hurrying, rats carrying papers. As Mrs. Frisby stepped from the elevator, it became obvious that strangers were a rarity down there, for the hubbub of a dozen conversations stopped abruptly, and all heads turned to look at her. They did not look hostile, nor were they alarmed—since her two companions were familiar to them—but merely curious. Then, as quickly as it had died out, the sound of talking began again, as if the rats were too polite to stand and stare. But one of them, a lean rat with a scarred face, left his group and walked toward them.

"Justin. Mr. Ages. And I see we have a guest." He spoke graciously, with an air of quiet dignity, and Mrs. Frisby noticed two more things about him. First, the scar on his face ran across his left eye, and over this eye he wore a black patch, fastened by a cord around his head. Second, he carried a satchel—rather like a hand-bag—by a strap over his shoulders.

"A guest whose name you will recognize," said Justin. "She is Mrs. Jonathan Frisby. Mrs. Frisby, this is Nicodemus."

"A name I recognize indeed," said the rat called Nicodemus. "Mrs. Frisby—are you perhaps aware of this?—your late husband was one of our greatest friends. You are welcome here."

"Thank you," said Mrs. Frisby, but she was more puzzled than ever. "In fact, I did not know that you knew my husband. But I'm glad to hear it, because I've come to ask your help."

"Mrs. Frisby has a problem," said Mr. Ages. "An urgent one."

"If we can help you, we will," said Nicodemus. He asked Mr. Ages: "Can it wait until after the meeting? An hour? We were just ready to begin again."

Mr. Ages considered. "An hour will make no difference, I think."

Nicodemus said: "Justin, show Mrs. Frisby to the library, where she can be comfortable until the meeting is over."

By this time the last of the other assembled rats had made their way into a large meeting hall, where they sat facing the raised platform. Nicodemus followed them, pulling some papers and a small reading glass from the satchel at his side as he walked to the front of the room.

Justin led Mrs. Frisby in another direction, down a corridor to their left, and again she had the impression of a faint, cool breeze against her face. She realized that the corridor she had walked in up above was merely a long entranceway, and that the halls around her were the rats' real living quarters. The one down which Justin led her was lined with doors, one of which he opened.

"In here," he said.

The room they entered was big, square, well lit, and had a faint musty smell. "It's reasonably comfortable, and if you like to read . . ." he gestured at the walls. They were lined with shelves from floor to ceiling, and on the shelves stood—Mrs. Frisby dredged in her memory. "Books," she said. "They're books."

"Yes," said Justin. "Do you read much?"

"Only a little," said Mrs. Frisby. "My husband taught me. And the children . . ." She started to tell him how. Laboriously scratching letters in the earth with a stick —it seemed so long ago. But Justin was leaving.

"Excuse me—I've got to go to the meeting. I hate meetings, but this one's important. We're finishing up the schedule for the Plan." He pronounced it with a capital P.

"The Plan?"

But he was out the door, closing it gently behind him.

Mrs. Frisby looked around her. The room—the library, Nicodemus had called it—had, in addition to its shelves of books, several tables with benches beside them, and on these were stacked more books, some of them open.

Books. Her husband, Jonathan, had told her about them. He had taught her and the children to read (the children had mastered it quickly, but she herself could barely manage the simplest words; she had thought perhaps it was because she was older). He had also told her about electricity. He had known these things—and so, it emerged, did the rats. It had never occurred to her until

81

now to wonder *how* he knew them. He had always known so many things, and she had accepted that as a matter of course. But who had taught him to read? Strangely, it also emerged that he had known the rats. Had they taught him? What had been his connection with them? She remembered his long visits with Mr. Ages. And Mr. Ages knew the rats, too.

She sighed. Perhaps when the meeting was over and she had had a chance to talk to Nicodemus—and had told him about Timothy and Moving Day—perhaps when that was settled, he could explain all this to her.

She noticed at the far end of the room a section of wall where there were no bookshelves. There was, instead, a blackboard, covered with words and numbers written in white chalk. There were pieces of chalk and an eraser in a rack at the bottom of it. The blackboard stood near the end of the longest of the tables. Was the library also used as a classroom? When she looked at the blackboard and, rather laboriously, read what was written on it, she saw that it was not. It was, rather, a conference room.

At the top of the board, in large letters, were printed the words:

THE PLAN OF THE RATS OF NIMH.

Isabella

Mrs. Frisby spelled it out slowly: The Plan of the Rats of Nimh. What, or where, was Nimh? The name had a strange and faraway sound. Had these rats, then, come here from someplace else? Did that explain why they had books and electric lights and wires and an electric motor? Yet they had been here—or at least there had been rats here—for as long as she could remember. Still, that was not so very long.

She wondered what other things they had. Suddenly she had an almost overwhelming desire to look around—to see what was behind the other doors and down the other corridors. She went to the door, opened it, and looked out into the hall. It was entirely deserted and silent, except that when she listened carefully she could hear a faint humming in the distance, as if something were running—another motor?

She started out into the hall, and then changed her mind. Better not. Nicodemus had been friendly—they had all been friendly—but explicit. He had said she was to wait in the library. And she was not there to pry but to get help. She went back into the library, closed the door, and sat on one of the benches. The books on the table were mostly paperbacks—small enough so that the rats could handle them easily enough, but too big for her; so she sat in front of the blackboard and looked at it again.

Beneath the title across the top, in neatly chalked handwriting, were columns of words and figures:

Schedule

January:

Group 1 (10):	Oats.	30 loads = 2 bu.
Group 2 (10):	Wheat.	30 loads = 2 bu.
Group 3 (10):	Corn.	20 loads = 1½ bu.
Group 4 (10):	Misc. seeds	Est. 10 loads total

The rest of the blackboard was filled with more rows of figures, each headed by the name of a month: February, March, April, May, and so on through July. At the bottom a separate square was ruled off:

Plows (Arthur's group) (14)
Plow No. 2. Complete: Jan. 1

Plow No. 3. Complete: Feb. 10
Plow No. 4. Complete: Mar. 20

Mrs. Frisby stared at all this, trying to make head or tail of it, but she could not. It was quite incomprehensible.

She was still puzzling over it when the door opened and a rat came in. It was a girl-rat, small and quite young, judging by her looks. She was carrying a pencil and some papers and looking at the papers as she walked, so that she did not see Mrs. Frisby at first. When she did she gasped and dropped the papers, scattering them on the floor. Her eyes opened wide.

"Who are you?" she asked. "I don't know you. How did you get in?" She backed toward the door.

"It's all right," said Mrs. Frisby. "I'm a friend of Mr. Ages." The rat was very young indeed, only a child.

"But why are you in here? Who let you in?"

"Nicodemus. He told me to wait here."

The girl-rat looked doubtful. "You might be a spy."

"A spy! How could I be? A spy from where?"

"I don't know. From outside. Maybe from Nimh?"

"I don't even know what Nimh is."

"That's what you *say*."

"But I don't. What is it?" asked Mrs. Frisby, feeling slightly annoyed.

"It's a place." The girl-rat, her alarm apparently subsiding, began picking up her scattered papers. "I'm supposed to be practicing my reading."

"What kind of a place?"

"It's where we came from. I don't know too much about it. I've never been there."

"How can you come from there if you've never been there?"

"My father and mother did. I was born afterward. I think it's white. Anyway, I know one thing. We don't want to go back. We don't want to get caught."

So, Mrs. Frisby thought—that sounds as if, whatever Nimh was, the rats had escaped from it to come here. But she realized that she was not likely to get very clear information from such a child. Again, she hoped that Nicodemus would explain it.

"Did Nicodemus come from Nimh, too?"

"Yes."

"And Justin?"

"Yes. You know Justin?"

"Yes."

86

"I guess you're not a spy," said the girl-rat. She sounded mildly disappointed. Then she added irrelevantly: "Justin's not married." She climbed on one of the benches and opened a book. "He's the best one of all. He's not even afraid of Dragon." She read in the book for perhaps thirty seconds, picked up her pencil, then put it down again. "I'm too young to get married."

"I suppose so," said Mrs. Frisby. "For a while yet. But that won't last long."

"That's what my mother says. But it *seems* long. And Justin might marry somebody else."

"Maybe not," said Mrs. Frisby, who could see beyond the tip of her nose. "He's pretty young himself yet. What's your name?"

"Isabella."

"It's a pretty name."

"It's all right. Only my brother calls me Izzy. I don't like that."

"I don't wonder. Where's your brother?"

"At the meeting. He's older. All the men are at the meeting. But my mother didn't go. The mothers don't always go. She's in the grain room, packing grain."

"Packing grain?"

"For the Plan. She doesn't like the Plan, though."

The Plan again.

"What is the Plan? Why doesn't she like it?"

"It's just—the Plan. For where we're going to live and all that. She doesn't like it because she says it's too hard —no more electric lights, no more refrigerator, no more running water. But she isn't deserting or anything. Not like Jenner. We didn't like Jenner."

"Who's Jenner?"

"He was in the group, but he quit. Maybe he went back to Nimh. We don't know."

Mrs. Frisby was gradually getting a picture of life in the rat colony—a somewhat confusing one because Isabella was a child, but nonetheless certain things were apparent: They had a grain room (presumably for food storage); the females sometimes went to meetings and sometimes not; Nicodemus seemed to be the leader; they had a Plan for the future that some rats did not like; and one, named Jenner, had deserted. Or had others gone with him? She was about to ask Isabella when the library door opened and Nicodemus, Justin, and Mr. Ages entered. Another rat came with them, a stranger.

A Powder
for Dragon

The strange rat was named Arthur. He was stocky, square and muscular, with bright, hard eyes. He looked efficient.

"You might call him our chief engineer," said Nicodemus to Mrs. Frisby, "as, indeed, you might call Justin the captain of the guard—if we had any such titles, but we don't. Mr. Ages thought Arthur should come along, though he didn't say why. So we still don't know what your problem is."

Isabella was gone. She had dropped her papers on the floor again when the others had entered, and Justin, to her intense confusion and visible delight, had helped her pick them up.

"Hello, Izzy," he had said. "How's the reading coming?"

"It's fine," she said. "I finished the Third Reader last week. Now I'm on the Fourth."

"The Fourth Reader already! You're getting quite grown up!" At that she had almost dropped the papers a third time and made a dash for the door. It did not matter, Mrs. Frisby noticed, if Justin called her Izzy—just so he called her something.

Nicodemus closed the door behind her, then sat down on one of the benches, facing Mrs. Frisby; the others sat down, too, Mr. Ages stretching his splinted leg in front of him. Nicodemus took the reading glass from his satchel, opened it, and through it gravely examined Mrs. Frisby's face. "You will forgive the glass and the scrutiny," he said. "When I lost my left eye, I also damaged the right one; I can see little close-up without the glass—indeed, not very much even with it." At length he folded the glass and put it on the table.

"Now," he said, "what is it we can do to help you?"

So Mrs. Frisby recounted once more the events that had led to her coming there, and at the end repeated what the owl had advised her to say—"move the house into the lee of the stone."

She added: "I don't understand just what he meant by that. Jeremy—the crow—says it means the side where there's no wind. But what good would that do?"

"I think I know what he meant," said Nicodemus. "In a broad sense, lee means the sheltered side. A bird, flying over Mrs. Fitzgibbon's garden, would notice something most of us would miss."

90

He reached into his satchel and took out a sheet of paper and a pencil; he opened the reading glass again. As he talked, he drew a sketch:

"When a farmer plows a field with a big rock in it, he plows around the rock—close on each side, but leaving a triangle of unplowed land on each end.

"Mrs. Frisby's house is beside the rock, and will get plowed up—and probably crushed, as the owl said. But if we can move it a few feet—so that it lies buried *behind* the rock—in the lee—then she and her children can stay in it as long as they need to.

"From the air, the way the owl sees it, the garden would look like this." He inspected the sketch through the reading glass and then placed it on the table.

Mrs. Frisby climbed up on the bench and looked at it. It was a rough map, showing the garden, the big stone near the middle, and the way the furrows made by the plow would curve around it, rather like waves around a boat.

"Show me where your house is buried," said Nicodemus. Mrs. Frisby pointed to the spot on the sketch.

"I know where that cinder block is," said the rat named Arthur. "In fact, I thought about bringing it in, but I decided it was too long a haul. They had it tied on top of the harrow for weight, and it fell off just as they were finishing the garden."

"Can you move it," asked Nicodemus, pointing at the sketch, "to this spot right here, and bury it again?"

"Yes," said Arthur. "That shouldn't be hard."

Mrs. Frisby was delighted; looking at the map, it all became clear, and she could see what a beautifully simple idea it was. When Mr. Fitzgibbon plowed, he

would go right past their house; they would not have to move until Timothy was well and until the weather was truly warm. She remembered again what her husband had said—how easy to unlock a door when you have the key. She had found the key. Or rather, the owl had found it.

Nicodemus asked Arthur: "How long will it take?"

"Depends. With a party of ten, a couple of hours. With twenty, maybe an hour."

"We can spare twenty. But it's still too long." He looked worried.

So did Arthur. "Yes," he said. "We'll have to work at night—but even so . . . There's just no cover at all. It's wide open."

92

"We'll have to take care of Dragon," said Justin.

"Yes," said Mr. Ages, "and with this leg, I can't do it. I'd never make it to the bowl, much less get back again."

Mrs. Frisby, looking at their baffled faces, felt her delight subsiding. Obviously something was wrong.

"I don't understand," she said. "I know about Dragon, of course, but . . ."

"At night," said Justin, "Dragon prowls the farmyard like a tiger. And you don't see him until he's on top of you."

"Then you can't move my house after all."

"Well," Justin said, "ordinarily . . ." He turned to Nicodemus. "Should I explain it to her?"

"Yes," said Nicodemus.

"Ordinarily," said Justin, "when we have a long project to do at night—sometimes even by day—we make sure Dragon won't bother us: We put sleeping powder in his food. Mr. Ages makes it. It doesn't do the cat any harm; but he stays extremely drowsy for the next eight hours or so. We station a sentry to watch him, and we're free to work."

"You did it yesterday!" cried Mrs. Frisby, remembering the figures toiling the wire through the grass, remembering how strangely disinterested Dragon had seemed when he saw her. "I saw the cat sleeping in the yard."

"Yes," said Justin, "but today Mr. Ages has a broken leg."

"Then he can't make the powder?"

"It isn't that," said Mr. Ages. "I've plenty of the powder."

"The trouble is," said Justin, "it's Mr. Ages who puts

it in Dragon's dinner bowl, inside the farm kitchen. With his leg broken, he can't move fast enough."

"But why Mr. Ages?" said Mrs. Frisby. "Can't someone else do it?"

"I'd be glad to do it myself," said Justin, "but I'm too big."

"You see," Nicodemus explained, "Mrs. Fitzgibbon feeds the cat in the morning and in the evening, and his bowl is always kept in the same place—next to a cabinet in one corner of the kitchen. There's a very shallow space between the floor and the bottom of the cabinet. A few years ago when we conceived the idea of putting Dragon to sleep, we cut a hole in the floor just behind the cabinet —if we put it anywhere else they'd see it. To reach the bowl, Mr. Ages crawls under the cabinet. When he gets to the edge, he makes a quick dash to the bowl, drops in the powder, and dashes back out of sight. But with a broken leg, he can't dash."

"We might try leaving some bait outside the house," said Justin. "That worked once."

"Once out of a dozen tries," said Nicodemus. "It isn't dependable, and we don't have much time. To be safe, we ought to move that block tonight."

"If we had some catfood . . ." said Justin, thinking aloud. "He might eat that, even on the porch, because he knows it's his. Maybe tonight I could go in through the attic and down to the kitchen . . ."

"No use," said Mr. Ages. "They keep it in a metal cabinet up on the wall. You couldn't get it without a crew. And that would make too much noise."

"Anyway," said Nicodemus, "it would put off moving the block until tomorrow night."

"Then," Justin said, "I guess what we do is stake out scouts wherever we can, try to keep track of Dragon, and hope for the best. Some nights he doesn't go near the garden at all. We might be lucky."

"Or we might not," said Arthur. "I don't like it. We can't dig that block out without some noise, you know."

Mrs. Frisby interrupted quietly. "There is another way," she said. "If Mr. Ages can get into the kitchen, so can I. If you will give me the powder and show me the way, I will try to put it in Dragon's bowl."

Justin said quickly: "No. It's no job for a lady."

"You forget," Mrs. Frisby said, "I'm Timothy's mother. If you, and Arthur, and others in your group can take risks to save him, surely I can, too. And consider this: I don't want any of you to be hurt—maybe even killed—by Dragon. But even more, I don't want the attempt to fail. Perhaps the worst that will happen to you, with luck, is that you will have to scatter and run, and leave my house unmoved. But then what will happen to us? Timothy, at least, will die. So if there is no one else to put the cat to sleep, I must do it."

Nicodemus considered, and then spoke:

"She's right, of course. If she chooses to take the risk, we can't deny her the right." To Mrs. Frisby he added: "But you should know that the danger is great. It was in the same kitchen, yesterday, running from Dragon's bowl, that Mr. Ages got his leg broken. And it was in doing the same thing, last year, that your husband died."

The Marketplace

Mrs. Frisby's head was buried in her arms. "I never knew," she said. "All I knew was that he didn't come back. But I never knew what happened. I didn't even know he knew you. Why didn't he ever tell me?"

Justin touched her shoulder gently. "It's hard for you to learn it this way, so suddenly," he said. "We thought about telling you when it happened, but we decided we shouldn't. It wouldn't have done any good."

"You ask why Jonathan never told you about us," Nicodemus added. "He had a reason, a good one. Still he worried about it a lot, and he might have told you in the end. But then it was too late."

96

"What was the reason?" Mrs. Frisby raised her face. There were tears on her cheeks, but she had stopped crying.

"To answer that I would have to tell you quite a long story—the whole story about us, and Nimh, and Jonathan, and how we came here. He came with us, you see. I don't mind doing that, but I don't know if there is time now."

"I think there is," said Justin, "if Mr. Ages and I go to get the powder while you're telling it."

"With this leg," said Mr. Ages glumly, "that will take long enough to tell it twice."

"I had forgotten," said Justin contritely. "Would it be better if I went alone?"

"No," said Mr. Ages. "There are so many different powders in my storeroom. You wouldn't know which to bring back. I'll go with you. But we'll go slowly."

"And I," said Arthur, "will see about the equipment for tonight. We'll need shovels, crowbars, block and tackle, rollers . . ." He left, still listing tools.

Nicodemus said to Mrs. Frisby, "I think that we, too, should leave the library. There will be others coming in, like Isabella, to practice reading, and some to do research."

"Research?"

"We've got some new books on agriculture—farming, gardening, fertilizing, things like that—and we're studying them. It's part of the Plan."

"I don't know what the Plan is."

"No," agreed Nicodemus, "but when I've told you our story, you'll understand that, too."

He opened the door and led Mrs. Frisby down the

corridor past several more doors, all closed. He stopped
before one, which he opened.

"My office," he said. "Please come in."

The room she entered was smaller than the library, but
much more comfortably—almost elegantly—furnished.
There was a rug on the floor (the same pattern, she
noticed, as the carpet in the hallway above), a light recessed in the ceiling and another in the wall next to a
table. There were bookshelves; on one shelf an electric
clock hummed quietly to itself. A book lay open on the
table, with a chair in front of it; against the opposite
wall stood a small sofa, neatly upholstered in cloth.
But what attracted Mrs. Frisby's attention most was a
box in one corner of the room, a box with dials and a

small light shining on the front; from this box came the soft sound of music. She listened entranced.

"You like music?" said Nicodemus. "So do I."

"That must be a radio." Again, something vaguely remembered from what Jonathan had once told her. Music. She had heard it only two or three times in her life, when the Fitzgibbons had left a window open and someone was playing inside. And never up close. It was a lovely sound.

"Yes," said Nicodemus. "We didn't get it for music, of course, but to hear the news. Still as long as it's here—why not use it?"

He sat down, and so did Mrs. Frisby.

"Now," he said, "I will tell you about Nimh. You'll be interested, I think, because your husband was part of it. And when I'm finished, I think you will see why he felt he could not tell you himself."

The story begins (Nicodemus continued) not at Nimh, but at a marketplace on the edge of a big city. It was called the Farmers' Market, a great square of a place with a roof over part of it and no walls to speak of. There early every morning the farmers arrived from all over the surrounding countryside, with trucks full of tomatoes, corn, cabbages, potatoes, eggs, chickens, hams, food for the city. One part of it was reserved for the fishermen who brought crabs and oysters and bass and flounders. It was a fine place, noisy and full of smells.

We lived near this market—my father, my mother, my nine sisters and brothers and I—underground in a big pipe that had once been part of a storm sewer, but was no longer used. There were hundreds of other rats

99

in the neighborhood. It was a rough life, but not so hard as you might think, because of the market.

Every evening at five o'clock the farmers and the fishermen would close up their stalls, pack their trucks, and go home. At night, hours later, the cleanup men would arrive with brooms and hoses. But in between, the market was ours. The food the farmers left behind! Peas and beans that fell from the trucks, tomatoes and squashes, pieces of meat and fish trimmed as waste—they lay on the sidewalks and in the gutters; they filled great cans that were supposed to be covered but seldom were. There was always ten times more than we could eat, and so there was never any need for fighting over it.

Fighting? Quite the contrary, the marketplace was a perfect place for playing, and so we did, the young rats at least, as soon as we had finished eating. There were empty boxes for hide-and-seek, there were walls to climb, tin cans to roll, and pieces of twine to tie and swing on. There was even, in the middle of the square, a fountain to swim in when the weather was hot. Then, at the first clang of the cleanup men in the distance, one of the older rats would sound a warning, and everyone would pick up as much food as he could to carry home. All of us kept a reserve supply, because some days— Sundays and holidays—the market would be closed, and we were never quite sure when this would happen.

When I went to the market, it was usually with two companions, my older brother Gerald and a friend of ours named Jenner. These were my two closest friends; we liked the same games, the same jokes, the same topics of conversation—even the same kinds of food. I particularly admired Jenner, who was extremely quick and intelligent.

One evening in early fall Jenner and I set out for the marketplace. It must have been September, for the leaves were just turning yellow and some children were throwing a football in a vacant lot. Gerald had to stay home that night; he had caught a cold, and since the air was chilly, my mother thought he should not go out. So Jenner and I went without him. I remember we promised to bring him back some of his favorite food, beef liver, if we could find any.

We took our usual route to the market, not along the streets but through the narrow walkways between the buildings, mostly commercial warehouses and garages, that bordered the square. As we walked, we were joined by more rats; at that time of day they converged on the marketplace from all directions. When we reached the square, I noticed that there was a white truck of an odd, square shape parked on the street bordering it, perhaps a block away. I say I noticed it—I did not pay any particular attention to it, for trucks were common enough in that part of town; but if I had, I would have noticed that printed on each side of it were four small letters: NIMH. I would not have known what they were, of course, for at that time neither I nor any of the other rats knew how to read.

It was growing dark when we reached the market, but through the dusk we could see that there was an unusually large supply of food—a great mound of it—near the center of the square, away from the roofed-over portion. I suppose that should have served as a warning, but it didn't. I remember Jenner's saying, "They must have had a really busy day," and we ran joyfully toward the pile along with several dozen other rats.

Just as we reached the food it happened. All around us suddenly there was shouting. Bright, blinding searchlights flashed on, aimed at us and at the mound of food, so that when we tried to run away from it, we could not see where we were going. Between and behind the lights there were shadows moving swiftly, and as they came toward us I could see that they were men—men in white uniforms carrying nets, round nets with long handles.

"Look out!" cried Jenner. "They're trying to catch us." He darted in one direction, I in another, and I lost sight of him.

We all ran—straight toward the men with the nets. There was no other way to run; they had us encircled. The nets flailed down, scooped, flailed again. I suppose some rats made it through, slipping between the men and past the lights. I felt a swish—a net just missed me. I turned and ran back toward the mound, thinking I might hide myself in it. But then came another swish, and that time I felt the enveloping fibers fall over me. They entangled my legs, then my neck. I was lifted from the ground along with three other rats, and the net closed around us.

In the Cage

Mrs. Frisby said: "But why did they want to catch you? And how did you ever get away again?"

"At first," said Nicodemus, "I thought it must be because they didn't like our stealing the food. And yet you could hardly even call it stealing—it was waste food, and all they did with it was haul it away to the city incinerator. So what harm if we ate some of it? Of course, there are people who just dislike rats, whether they're doing any harm or not."

"And mice, too," said Mrs. Frisby.

"True," said Nicodemus. "Though not so much as rats, I think. Anyway, that wasn't the reason at all; but what the real reason was, I didn't find out for a while. As to getting away—that, too, didn't happen until much later."

No, I was firmly and inextricably caught, snared in the net and helpless (Nicodemus continued). When the man who held it saw that he had four rats, he pulled a draw string that closed it up. He put the net down and picked up another, an empty one. He moved on into the square, leaving us to lie there. I tried gnawing my way out, but the strands were made of some kind of plastic, as hard as wire.

The noise and movement began to die down eventually; I supposed the rats in the square had all either been caught or had escaped. I heard one man call to another: "I guess that's the lot." Someone else was turning a light this way and that, searching the rest of the market area.

"Not a one to be seen."

"We could hide and wait for another wave."

"There won't be another wave. Not tonight. Probably not for four or five nights."

"Word gets around."

"You mean they communicate?" A third voice.

"You bet they communicate. And the next time they do come, you can be sure they'll case the place carefully. We were lucky. These rats hadn't been bothered for years. They'd grown careless."

"How many did the lab order?" Someone was turning out the lights one at a time.

"Five dozen. How many have we got?"

"About that. Maybe more."

"Let's load the truck."

In a minute or so I felt myself being lifted up; and swinging back and forth in the net, I was carried with my three companions to the white truck I had seen earlier. Its back doors were open, and it was lighted inside. I could see that its whole interior was a large wire cage. Into this our net was thrust; the man then opened the draw string and we were dumped onto the floor, which was covered with sawdust. The other nets were emptied one at a time the same way; and in a few minutes there was a good-sized crowd of us on the floor, all more or less dazed and all (if I was typical) terrified. The cage was locked, the doors clanged shut, and the lights went out. I heard the truck motor start; a second later the floor lurched beneath me. We were moving. Where were they taking us? For what purpose?

Then, in the dark, I heard a voice beside me.

"Nicodemus?" It was Jenner. You can imagine how glad I was to hear him. But I was sorry, too.

"Jenner. I thought maybe you got away."

"I was in the last net. I thought I saw you across the floor."

"Where are we going?"

"I don't know."

"What's a lab?"

"A laboratory."

"Yes, but what is it?"

"I don't know. I've just heard the word somewhere."

"Well, I think that's where we're going. Whatever it is."

The truck rumbled along through the dark, over bumpy streets at first, then, at a higher speed, over a smooth highway. There were no windows in the back, so it was impossible to see where we were going—not that I would have known anyway, never before having been more than half a dozen blocks from home. I think we drove for about two hours, but it might have been less, before the truck slowed, and turned, and finally came to a stop.

The back doors were opened again, and through the wire wall of the cage I saw that we had come to a building, very modern, of white cement and glass. It was square and big, about ten stories tall. Night had fallen, and most of its windows were dark, but the platform to which our truck drove us was lighted, and there were people waiting for us.

A door opened, and three men came out. One of them pushed a cart, a hand truck piled with small wire cages. The man beside him was dressed in a heavy coat, boots, and thick leather gloves. The third man wore heavy horn-rimmed glasses and a white coat. He was obviously the leader.

The men from the truck, the ones who had caught us, now joined the men from the building.

"How many did you get?" asked the man in the white coat.

"Hard to count—they keep moving around. But I make it between sixty and seventy."

"Good. Any trouble?"

"No. It was easy. They acted almost tame."

"I hope not. I've got enough tame ones."

"Oh, they're lively enough. And they look healthy."

"Let's get them out."

The man with the gloves and the boots then donned a wire face-mask as well, and climbed in among us. He opened a small sliding trapdoor at the back of our cage; a man outside held one of the small cages up to the opening, and one at a time we were pushed out into our individual little prisons. A few of the rats snarled and tried to bite; I did not, and neither did Jenner; it was too obviously futile. When it was finished, the man in the white coat said, "Sixty-three—good work." A man from the truck said, "Thanks, Dr. Schultz." And we were racked on the hand truck and wheeled into the building.

Dr. Schultz. I did not know it then, but I was to be his prisoner (and his pupil) for the next three years.

We spent the rest of that night in a long white room. It was, in fact, a laboratory, with a lot of equipment at one end that I didn't understand at all then—bottles and shiny metal things and black boxes with wires trailing from them. But our end held only rows of cages on shelves, each cage with a tag on it, and each separated from its neighbors by wooden partitions on both sides. Someone came around with a stack of small jars and fastened one to my cage; a little pipe led through the bars like a sipping straw—drinking water. Then the lights were dimmed and we were left alone.

That cage was my home for a long time. It was not uncomfortable; it had a floor of some kind of plastic, medium soft and warm to the touch; with wire walls and ceiling, it was airy enough. Yet just the fact that it was a cage made it horrible. I, who had always run where I wanted, could go three hops forward, three hops back again, and that was all. But worse was the dreadful feeling—I know we all had it—that we were completely at the mercy of someone we knew not at all, for some purpose we could not guess. What were their plans for us?

As it turned out, the uncertainty itself was the worst suffering we had to undergo. We were treated well enough, except for some very small, very quick flashes of pain, which were part of our training. And we were always well fed, though the food, scientifically compiled pellets, was not what you'd call delicious.

But of course we didn't know that when we arrived, and I doubt that any of us got much sleep that first night. I know I didn't. So, in a way, it was a relief when early the next morning the lights snapped on and Dr. Schultz entered. There were two other people with him, a young man and a young woman. Like him, they were dressed in white laboratory coats. He was talking to them as they entered the room and walked toward our cages.

". . . three groups. Twenty for training on injection series A, twenty on series B. That will leave twenty-three for the control group. They get no injections at all—except, to keep the test exactly even, we will prick them with a plain needle. Let's call the groups A, B, and C for control; tag them and number them A-1 through A-20, B-1 through B-20, and so on. Number the cages the same way, and keep each rat in the same cage throughout. Diet will be the same for all."

"When do we start the injections?"

"As soon as we're through with the tagging. We'll do that now. George, you number the tags and the cages. Julie, you tie them on. I'll hold."

So the young woman's name was Julie; the young man was George. They all put gloves on, long, tough

plastic ones that came to their elbows. One by one we were taken from our cages, held gently but firmly by Dr. Schultz while Julie fastened around each of our necks a narrow ribbon of yellow plastic bearing a number. I learned eventually that mine was number A-10.

They were kind, especially Julie. I remember that when one rat was being tagged, she looked at it and said, "Poor little thing, he's frightened. Look how he's trembling."

"What kind of biologist are you?" said Dr. Schultz. "The 'poor little thing' is a she, not a he."

When my turn came, the door of my cage slid open just enough for Dr. Schultz to put his gloved hand through. I cowered to the back of the cage, which was just what he expected me to do; one hand pressed me flat against the wire wall; then his fingers gripped my shoulders. The other hand held my head just behind the ears, and I was powerless. I was lifted from the cage and felt the plastic collar clipped around my neck. I was back inside with the door closed in less than a minute. The collar was not tight, but by no amount of tugging, twisting or shaking was I ever able to get it off.

I watched through the wire front of my cage as the others were caught and tagged. About six cages down from me, on the same shelf, I saw them put a collar on Jenner; but once he was back in his cage, I could see him no longer.

A little later in the morning they came around again, this time pushing a table on wheels. It was loaded with a bottle of some clear liquid, a long rack of sharp needles, and a plunger. Once more I was lifted from the cage. This time George did the holding while Dr.

Schultz fastened one of the needles to the plunger. I felt a sharp pain in my hip; then it was over. We all got used to that, for from then on we got injections at least twice a week. What they were injecting and why, I did not know. Yet for twenty of us those injections were to change our whole lives.

The Maze

During the days that followed, our lives fell into a pattern, and the reason for our captivity gradually became clear. Dr. Schultz was a neurologist—that is, an expert on brains, nerves, intelligence, and how people learn things. He hoped, by experimenting on us, to find out whether certain injections could help us to learn more and faster. The two younger people working with him, George and Julie, were graduate students in biology.

"Watch always," he told them, "for signs of improvement, faster learning, quicker reaction in group A as compared to group B, and both as compared to the control group."

My own training began on the day after the first injections. It was George who did it; I suppose Julie and Dr. Schultz were doing the same test on other rats. He took my cage from the shelf and carried it to another room, similar to the first one but with more equipment in it, and no shelves of cages. He placed the cage in a slot against a wall, slid open the end, opened a matching door in the wall—and I was free.

Or so I thought. The small doorway in the wall led into a short corridor, which opened, or seemed to, dirictly onto a green lawn. I could see it clearly, and behind it some bushes, and behind them a street—all outdoors, and nothing but air between me and them. Furthermore, I could smell the fresh outdoor breeze blowing in. Were they letting me go?

I made a dash toward the open end of the corridor— and then jumped back. I could not go on. About two feet from my cage (still open behind me) there was something dreadfully wrong with the floor. When I touched my feet to it, a terrible, prickling feeling came over my skin, my muscles cramped, my eyes blurred and I got instantly dizzy. I never got used to that feeling—no one ever does—but I did experience it many times, and eventually learned what it was: electric shock. It is not exactly a pain, but it is unbearable.

Yet I was in a frenzy to reach that open lawn, to run for the bushes, to get away from the cage. I tried again —and jumped back again. No use. Then I saw, leading off to the left, another corridor. I had not noticed it at first because I had been looking so eagerly at the open end of the one I was in. The second one seemed to stop about five feet away in a blank wall. Yet there was light there: it must turn a corner. I ran down it, cautiously, not trusting the floor. At the end it turned right—and there was the lawn again, another opening. I got closer that time; then, just as I thought I was going to make it —another shock. I pulled back and saw that there was still another corridor, leading off to the right. Again I ran, again I saw the open escape hole, and again I was stopped by shock. This was repeated over and over; yet each time I seemed to get a little closer to freedom.

But when finally I reached it and the grass was only a step away, a wire wall snapped down in front of me, another behind me; the ceiling opened above me and a gloved hand reached in and picked me up.

A voice said: "Four minutes, thirty-seven seconds."

It was George.

I had, after all my running through the corridors, emerged into a trap only a few feet from where I had started, and through a concealed opening up above, George had been watching everything I did.

I had been in what is called a maze, a device to test intelligence and memory. I was put in it many times again, and so were the others. The second time I got through it a little faster, because I remembered—to some extent—which corridors had electric floors and which did not. The third time I was still faster; and after each trial George (or sometimes Julie, sometimes Dr. Schultz) would write down how long it took. You might ask: Why would I bother to run through it at all, if I knew it was only a trick? The answer is I couldn't help it. When you've lived in a cage, you can't bear *not* to run, even if what you're running toward is an illusion.

There were more injections, and other kinds of tests, and some of these were more important than the maze, because the maze was designed only to find out how quickly we could learn, while some of the others actually taught us things—or at least led up to actual teaching.

One was what Dr. Schultz called "shape recognition." We would be put into a small room with three doors leading out—one round, one square, and one triangular. These doors were on hinges, with springs that held them shut, but they were easy to push open, and each door led into another room with three more doors like the first one. But the trick was this: If you went through the wrong door, the room you entered had an electric floor, and you got a shock. So you had to learn: In the first room, you used the round door; second room, triangle, and so on.

All of these activities helped to pass the time, and the weeks went by quickly, but they did not lessen our longing to get away. I wished for my old home in the storm sewer; I wished I could see my mother and father, and run with my brother to the marketplace. I know all the others felt the same way; yet it seemed a hopeless thing. Still there was one rat who decided to try it anyway.

He was a young rat, probably the youngest of all that had been caught, and by chance he was in the cage next to mine; I might mention that like Jenner and me, he was in the group Dr. Schultz called A. His name was Justin.

It was late one night that I heard him calling to me, speaking softly, around the wooden partition between our cages. Those partitions generally kept all of us from getting to know each other as well as we might have done, and discouraged us from talking much to one another; it was quite hard to hear around them, and of course you could never see the one you were talking to. I think Dr. Schultz had purposely had them made of some soundproof material. But you *could* hear, if you and your neighbor got in the corners of the cages nearest each other and spoke out through the wire front.

"Nicodemus?"

"Yes?" I went over to the corner.

"How long have we been here?"

"You mean since the beginning? Since we were caught?"

"Yes."

"I don't know. Several months—I think, but I have no way to keep track."

"I know. I don't either. Do you suppose it's winter outside now?"

"Probably. Or late fall."

"It will be cold."

"But not in here."

"No. But I'm going to try to get out."

"Get out? But how? Your cage is shut."

"Tomorrow we get injections, so they'll open it. When they do, I'm going to run."

"Run where?"

"I don't know. At least I'll get a look around. There might be some way out. What can I lose?"

"You might get hurt."

"I don't think so. Anyway *they* won't hurt me."

By they he meant Dr. Schultz and the other two. He

added confidently:

"All those shots, all the time they've spent—we're too valuable to them now. They'll be careful."

That idea had not occurred to me before, but when I thought about it, I decided he was right. Dr. Schultz, Julie and George had spent most of their working hours with us for months; they could not afford to let any harm come to us. On the other hand, neither could they afford to allow any of us to escape.

Justin made his attempt the next morning. And it did cause a certain amount of excitement, but not at all what we expected. It was Julie who opened Justin's cage with a hypodermic in her hand. Justin was out with a mighty leap, hit the floor (about four feet down) with a thump, shook himself and ran, disappearing from my view heading toward the other end of the room.

Julie seemed not at all alarmed. She calmly placed the needle on a shelf, then walked to the door of the laboratory and pushed a button on the wall near it. A red light came on over the door. She picked up a notebook and pencil from a desk near the door and followed Justin out of my sight.

A few minutes later Dr. Schultz and George entered. They opened the door cautiously and closed it behind them. "The outer door is shut, too," said Dr. Schultz. "Where is it?"

"Down here," said Julie, "inspecting the air ducts."

"Really? Which one is it?"

"It's one of the A group, just as you expected. Number nine. I'm keeping notes on it."

Obviously the red light was some kind of a warning signal, both outside the door and in—"laboratory animal

at large." And not only had Dr. Schultz known one of us was out, but he had expected it to happen.

". . . a few days sooner than I thought," he was saying, "but so much the better. Do you realize . . ."

"Look," said Julie. "He's doing the whole baseboard —but he's studying the windows, too. See how he steps back to look up?"

"Of course," said Dr. Schultz. "And at the same time he's watching us, too. Can't you see?"

"He's pretty cool about it," said George.

"Can you imagine one of the lab rats doing that? Or even one of the controls? We've got to try to grasp what we have on our hands. The A group is now three hundred per cent ahead of the control group in learning, and getting smarter all the time. B group is only twenty per cent ahead. It's the new DNA that's doing it. We have a real breakthrough, and since it is DNA, we may very well have a true mutation, a brand new species of rat. But we've got to be careful with it. I think we should go ahead now with the next injection series."

"The steroids?"

(Whatever that meant.)

"Yes. It may slow them up a little—though I doubt it. But even if it does, it will be worth it, because I'm betting it will increase their life span by double at least. Maybe more. Maybe *much* more."

"Look," said Julie, "A-9 has made a discovery. He's found the mice."

George said: "See how he's studying them."

"Probably," said Dr. Schultz wryly, "he's wondering if they're ready for their steroid injections, too. As a matter of fact, I think the G group is. They're doing almost as well as A group."

"Should I get the net and put him back?" George asked.

"I doubt that you'll need it," Dr. Schultz said, "now that he's learned he can't get out."

But they were underestimating Justin. He had learned no such thing.

A Lesson
in Reading

Of course, Justin did not escape that day, nor even that year. When they—Julie—put on a glove and went to pick him up, he submitted meekly enough, and in a short time he was back in his cage.

Yet he had learned some things. He had, as Julie noticed, examined the air ducts—the openings along the wall through which warm air flowed in winter, cool air in summer—and he had studied the windows. Mainly he had learned that he could, occasionally at least, jump from his cage and wander around without incurring any anger or injury. All of this, eventually, was important. For it was Justin, along with Jenner, who finally figured out how to get away. I had a part in it, too. But all that came later.

I won't go into details about the rest of our training except for one part of it that was the most useful of all. But in general, during the months that followed, two things were happening:

First, we were learning more than any rats ever had before, and were becoming more intelligent than any rats had ever been.

The second thing could be considered, from some points of view, even more important—and certainly more astonishing—than the first. Dr. Schultz (you will recall) had said that the new series of injections might increase our life span by double or more. Yet even he was not prepared for what happened. Perhaps it was the odd combination of both types of injections working together—I don't know, and neither did he. But the result was that as far as he could detect, in the A group the aging process seemed to stop almost completely.

For example—during the years we were in the laboratory, most of the rats in the control group grew old and sickly, and finally died; so did those in B group, for though they were getting injections, too, the formula was not the same as ours. But among the twenty of us in A group, no one could see any signs that we were growing older at all. Apparently (though we seldom saw them) the same thing was happening with the G group, the mice who were getting the same injections we were.

Dr. Schultz was greatly excited about this. "The short life span has always been a prime limiting factor in education," he told George and Julie. "If we can double it, and speed up the learning process at the same time, the possibilities are enormous." Double it! Even now, years later, years after the injections were stopped, we seem scarcely any older than we were then.

We could not detect either of these things ourselves. That is, we didn't *feel* any different, and since we had no contact with the other groups, we had no basis for comparison. All we had to go by was what Dr. Schultz said. He and the others were preparing a research paper about us—to be published in some scientific journal—so each morning he dictated the results of the previous day's tests into a tape recorder. We heard all of it, though there was a lot of technical stuff we couldn't understand, especially at first. Until the paper was published (he kept reminding George and Julie of this) the whole experiment was to be kept secret.

The one important phase of training began one day after weeks of really hard work at the "shape recognition" that I mentioned before. But this was different. For the first time they used sounds along with the shapes, and pictures, real pictures we could recognize. For example, one of the first and simplest of these exercises was a picture, a clear photograph, of a rat. I suppose they felt sure we would know what that was. This picture was shown on a screen, with a light behind it. Then, after I had looked at the picture and recognized it, a shape flashed on the screen under it—a sort of half circle and two straight lines, not like anything I had seen before. Then the voice began:

"Are."

"Are."

"Are."

It was Julie's voice, speaking very clearly, but it had a tinny sound—it was a record. After repeating "are" a dozen times or so, that particular shape disappeared and another one came on the screen, still under the picture of the rat. It was a triangle, with legs on it. And Julie's voice began again:

"Aiee."

"Aiee."

"Aiee."

When that shape disappeared a third one came on the screen. This one was a cross. Julie's voice said:

"Tea."

"Tea."

"Tea."

Then all three shapes appeared at once, and the record said:

"Are."

"Aiee."

"Tea."

"Rat."

You will already have recognized what was going on: they were teaching us to read. The symbols under the picture were the letters R-A-T. But the idea did not become clear to me, nor to any of us, for quite a long time. Because, of course, we didn't know what reading *was*.

Oh, we learned to recognize the shapes easily enough, and when I saw the rat picture I knew straight away what symbols would appear beneath it. In the same way, when the picture showed a cat, I knew the same shapes would appear, except the first one would be a half-circle, and Julie's voice would repeat: "See—see—

see." I even learned that when the photograph showed not one but several rats, a fourth shape would appear under it—a snaky line—and the sound with that one was "ess—ess—ess." But as to what all this was *for*, none of us had any inkling.

It was Jenner who finally figured it out. By this time we had developed a sort of system of communication, a simple enough thing, just passing spoken messages from one cage to the next, like passing notes in school. Justin, who was still next to me, called to me one day:

"Message for Nicodemus from Jenner. He says important."

"All right," I said, "what's the message?"

"Look at the shapes on the wall next to the door. He says to look carefully."

My cage, like Jenner's and those of the rest of A group, was close enough to the door so I could see what he meant: Near the doorway there was a large, square piece of white cardboard fastened to the wall—a sign. It was covered with an assortment of black markings to which I had never paid any attention (though they had been there ever since we arrived).

Now, for the first time, I looked at them carefully, and I grasped what Jenner had discovered.

The top line of black marks on the wall were instantly familiar: R-A-T-S; as soon as I saw them I thought of the picture that went with them; and as soon as I did that I was, for the first time, reading. Because, of course, that's what reading is: using symbols to suggest a picture or an idea. From that time on it gradually became clear to me what all these lessons were for, and once I understood the idea, I was eager to learn more. I could scarcely wait for the next lesson, and the next. The whole concept of reading was, to me at least, fascinating. I remember how proud I was when, months later, I was able to read and understand that whole sign. I read it hundreds of times, and I'll never forget it:

RATS MAY NOT BE REMOVED FROM THE LABORATORY WITHOUT WRITTEN PERMISSION. And at the bottom, in smaller letters, the word NIMH.

But then a puzzling thing came up, a thing we're still not sure about even now. Apparently Dr. Schultz, who was running the lessons, did not realize how well they were succeeding. He continued the training, with new words and new pictures every day; but the fact is, once we had grasped the idea and learned the different sounds each letter stood for, we leaped way ahead of him. I remember well, during one of the lessons, looking at a picture of a tree. Under it the letters flashed on: T-R-E-E. But in the photograph, though the tree was in the foreground, there was a building in the background, and a sign near it. I scarcely glanced at T-R-E-E, but concentrated instead on reading the sign. It said:

NIMH. PRIVATE PARKING BY PERMIT ONLY. RESERVED FOR DOCTORS AND STAFF. NO VISITOR PARKING. The building behind it, tall and white, looked very much like the building we were in.

I'm sure Dr. Schultz had plans for testing our reading ability. I could even guess, from the words he was teaching us, what the tests were going to be like. For example, he taught us "left," "right," "door," "food," "open," and so on. It was not hard to imagine the test: I would be placed in one chamber, my food in another. There would be two doors, and a sign saying: "For food, open door at right." Or something like that. Then if I—if all of us—moved unerringly toward the proper door, he would know we understood the sign.

As I said, I'm sure he planned to do this, but apparently he did not think we were ready for it yet. I think maybe he was even a little afraid to try it; because if he did it too soon, or if for any other reason it did not work, his experiment would be a failure. He wanted to be sure, and his caution was his undoing.

Justin announced one evening around the partition:

"I'm going to get out of my cage tonight and wander around a bit."

"How can you? It's locked."

"Yes. But did you notice, along the bottom edge there's a printed strip?"

I had not noticed it. I should perhaps explain that when Dr. Schultz and the others opened our cages we could never quite see how they did it; they manipulated something under the plastic floor, something we couldn't see.

"What does it say?"

"I've been trying to read it the last three times they brought me back from training. It's very small print. But I think I've finally made it out. It says: To release door, pull knob forward and slide right."

"Knob?"

"Under the floor, about an inch back, there's a metal thing just in front of the shelf. I think that's the knob, and I think I can reach it through the wire. Anyway,

I'm going to try."

"Now?"

"Not until they close up."

"Closing up" was a ritual Dr. Schultz, George and Julie went through each night. For about an hour they sat at their desks, wrote notes in books, filed papers in cabinets, and finally locked the cabinets. Then they checked all the cages, dimmed the lights, locked the doors and went home, leaving us alone in the still laboratory.

About half an hour after they left that night, Justin said: "I'm going to try now." I heard a scuffling noise, a click and scrape of metal, and in a matter of seconds I saw his door swing open. It was as simple as that—when you could read.

"Wait," I said.

"What's the matter?"

"If you jump down, you won't be able to get back in. Then they'll know."

"I thought of that. I'm not going to jump down. I'm going to climb up the outside of the cage. It's easy. I've climbed up the inside a thousand times. Above these cages there's another shelf, and it's empty. I'm going to

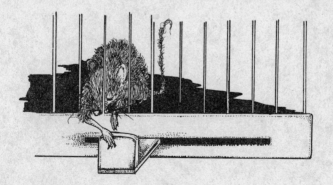

walk along there and see what I can see. I think there's a way to climb to the floor and up again."

"Why don't I go with you?" My door would open the same way as his.

"Better not this time, don't you think? If something goes wrong and I can't get back, they'll say: It's just A-9 again. But if two of us are found outside, they'll take it seriously. They might put new locks on the cages."

He was right, and you can see that already we both had the same idea in mind: that this might be the first step toward escape for all of us.

The Air Ducts

And so it was.

By teaching us how to read, they had taught us how to get away.

Justin climbed easily up the open door of his cage and vanished over the top with a flick of his tail. He came back an hour later, greatly excited and full of information. Yet it was typical of Justin that even excited as he was, he stayed calm, he thought clearly. He climbed down the front of my cage rather than his own, and spoke softly; we both assumed that by now the other rats were asleep.

"Nicodemus? Come on out. I'll show you how." He

directed me as I reached through the wire bars of the door and felt beneath it. I found the small metal knob, slid it forward and sideward, and felt the door swing loose against my shoulder. I followed him up the side of the cage to the shelf above. There we stopped. It was the first time I had met Justin face to face.

He said: "It's better talking here than around that partition."

"Yes. Did you get down?"

"Yes."

"How did you get back up?"

"At the end of this shelf there's a big cabinet—they keep the mouse cages in it. It has wire mesh doors. You can climb up and down them like a ladder."

"Of course," I said. "I remember now." I had seen that cabinet many times when my cage was carried past it. For some reason—perhaps because they were smaller —the mice were kept in cages-within-a-cage.

Justin said: "Nicodemus, I think I've found the way to get out."

"You have! How?"

"At each end of the room there's an opening in the baseboard at the bottom of the wall. Air blows in through one of them and out the other. Each one has a metal grid covering it, and on the grid there's a sign that says: Lift to adjust air flow. I lifted one of them; it hangs on hinges, like a trapdoor. Behind it there is a thing like a metal window—when you slide it wide open, more air blows in.

"But the main thing is, it's easily big enough to walk through and get out."

"But what's on the other side? Where does it lead?"

"On the other side there's a duct, a thing like a square metal pipe built right into the wall. I walked along it, not very far, but I can figure out where it must go. There's bound to be a duct like it leading to every room in the building, and they must all branch off one main central pipe—and that one has to lead, somewhere, to the outside. Because that's where our air comes from. That's why they never open the windows. I don't think those windows *can* open."

He was right, of course. The building had central air conditioning; what we had to do was find the main air shaft and explore it. There would have to be an intake at one end and an outlet at the other. But that was easier said than done, and before it was done there were questions to be answered. What about the rest of the rats? There were twenty of us in the laboratory, and we had to let the others know.

So, one by one, we woke them and showed them how to open their cages. It was an odd assembly that gathered that night, under the dimmed lights in the echoing laboratory, on the shelf where Justin and I had talked. We all knew each other in a way, from the passing of messages over the preceding months; yet except for Jenner and me, none of us had ever really met. We were strangers—though, as you can imagine, it did not take long for us to develop a feeling of comradeship, for we twenty were alone in a strange world. Just how alone and how strange none of us really understood at first; yet in a way we sensed it from the beginning. The group looked to me as leader, probably because it was Justin and I who first set them free, and because Justin was obviously younger than I.

We did not attempt to leave that night, but went together and looked at the metal grid Justin had discovered, and made plans for exploring the air ducts. Jenner was astute at that sort of thing; he could foresee problems.

"With a vent like this leading to every room," he said, "it will be easy to get lost. When we explore, we're going to need some way of finding our way back here."

"Why should we come back?" someone asked.

"Because it may take more than one night to find the way out. If it does, whoever is doing the exploring must be back in his cage by morning. Otherwise Dr. Schultz will find out."

Jenner was right. It took us about a week. What we did, after some more discussion, was to find some equipment: first, a large spool of thread in one of the cabinets where some of us had seen Julie place it one day. Second, a screwdriver that was kept on a shelf near the electric equipment—because, as Jenner pointed out, there would probably be a screen over the end of the air-shaft to keep out debris, and we might have to pry it loose. What we really needed was a light, for the ducts, at night, were completely dark. But there was none to be had, not even a box of matches. The thread and the screwdriver we hid in the duct, a few feet from the entrance. We could only hope they would not be missed, or that if they were, we wouldn't be suspected.

Justin and two others were chosen as the exploration party (one of the others was Arthur, whom you've met). They had a terrible time at first: Here was a maze to end all mazes; and in the dark they quickly lost their sense of direction. Still they kept at it, night after

night, exploring the network of shafts that laced like a cubical spiderweb through the walls and ceilings of the building. They would tie the end of their thread to the grid in our laboratory and unroll it from the spool as they went. Time and time again they reached the end of the thread and had to come back.

"It just isn't long enough," Justin would complain. "Every time I come to the end, I think: if I could just go ten feet farther . . ."

And finally, that's what he did. On the seventh night, just as the thread ran out, he and the other two reached a shaft that was wider than any they had found before, and it seemed, as they walked along it, to be slanting gently upward. But the spool was empty.

"You wait here," Justin said to the others. "I'm going just a little way farther. Hang on to the spool, and if I call, call back." (They had tied the end of the thread around the spool so they would not lose it in the dark.)

Justin had a hunch. The air coming through the shaft had a fresher smell where they were, and seemed to be blowing harder than in the other shafts. Up ahead he thought he could hear the whir of a machine running

133

quietly, and there was a faint vibration in the metal under his feet. He went on. The shaft turned upward at a sharp angle—and then, straight ahead, he saw it: a patch of lighter-colored darkness than the pitch black around him, and in the middle of it, three stars twinkling. It was the open sky. Across the opening there was, as Jenner had predicted, a coarse screen of heavy wire.

He ran toward it for a few seconds longer, and then stopped. The sound of the machine had grown suddenly louder, changing from a whir to a roar. It had, obviously, shifted speed; an automatic switch somewhere in the building had turned it from low to high, and the air blowing past Justin came on so hard it made him gasp. He braced his feet against the metal and held on. In a minute, as suddenly as it had roared, the machine returned to a whisper. He looked around and realized he was lucky to have stopped; by the dim light from the sky he could see that he had reached a point where perhaps two dozen air shafts came together like branches into the trunk of a tree. If he had gone a few steps farther he would never have been able to distinguish which shaft was his. He turned in his tracks, and in a few minutes he rejoined his friends.

We had a meeting that night, and Justin told all of us what he had found. He had left the thread, anchored by the screwdriver, to guide us out. Some were for leaving immediately, but it was late, and Jenner and I argued against it. We did not know how long it would take us to break through the screen at the end. If it should take more than an hour or two, daylight would be upon us. We would then be unable to risk returning to the laboratory, and would have to spend the day in the shaft—or try to get away by broad daylight. Dr. Schultz might even figure out how we had gone and trap us in the air shaft.

Finally, reluctantly, everyone agreed to spend one more day in the laboratory and leave early the next night. But it was a hard decision, with freedom so near and everyone thinking as I did: "Suppose . . ." Suppose Dr. Schultz grew suspicious and put locks on our cages? Suppose someone found our thread and pulled it out? (This was unlikely—the near end, tied to the spool, was six feet up the shaft, well hidden.) Just the same, we were uneasy.

Then, just as we were ending our meeting, a new complication arose. We had been standing in a rough circle on the floor of the laboratory, just outside the two screen doors that enclosed the mice cages. Now, from inside the cabinet, came a voice:

"Nicodemus." It was a clear but plaintive call, the voice of a mouse. We had almost forgotten the mice were there, and I was startled to hear that one of them knew my name. We all grew quiet.

"Who's calling me?" I asked.

"My name is Jonathan," said the voice. "We have been listening to your talk about going out. We would like to go, too, but we cannot open our cages."

As you can imagine, this caused a certain consternation, coming at the last minute. None of us knew much about the mice, except what we had heard Dr. Schultz dictate into his tape recorder. From that, we had learned only that they had been getting the same injections we were getting, and that the treatment had worked about as well on them as on us. They were a sort of side ex-

135

periment, without a control group.

Justin was studying the cabinet.

"Why not?" he said. "If we can get the doors open."

Someone muttered: "They'll slow us down."

"No," said the mouse Jonathan. "We will not. Only open our cages when you go, and we will make our own way. We won't even stay with you, if you prefer."

"How many are you?" I asked.

"Only eight. And the cabinet doors are easy to open. There's just a simple hook, half way up."

But Justin and Arthur had already figured that out. They climbed up the screen, unhooked the hook, and the doors swung open.

"The cages open the same way as yours," said another mouse, "but we can't reach far enough to unlatch them."

"All right," I said. "Tomorrow night, as soon as Dr. Schultz and the others leave, we'll open your cages, and you can follow the thread with us to get out. After that you're on your own."

"Agreed," said Jonathan, "and thank you."

"And now," I said, "we should all get back to the cages. Justin, please hook the doors again."

I had latched myself into my cage and was getting ready for sleep when I heard a scratching noise on the door, and there was Jenner, climbing down from above.

"Nicodemus," he said, "can I come in?"

"Of course. But it's getting on toward morning."

"I won't stay long." He unlatched the door and entered. "There's something we've got to decide."

"I know," I said. "I've been thinking about it, too."

"When we do get out, where are we going to go?"

136

I could not see Jenner's face in the dark of the cage, but I knew from his voice that he was worrying. I said:

"At first I thought, home, of course. But then, when I began remembering, I realized that won't work. We could find the way, I suppose, now that we can read. But if we did—what then? We wouldn't find anyone we know."

"And yet," Jenner said, "you know that's not the real point."

"No."

"The real point is this: We don't know where to go because we don't know what we are. Do you want to go back to living in a sewer-pipe? And eating other people's garbage? Because that's what rats do. But the fact is, we aren't rats any more. We're something Dr. Schultz has made. Something new. Dr. Schultz says our intelligence has increased more than one thousand per cent. I suspect he's underestimated; I think we're probably as intelligent as he is—maybe more. We can read, and with a little practice, we'll be able to write, too. I mean to do both. I think we can learn to do anything we want. But where do we do it? Where does a group of civilized rats fit in?"

"I don't know," I said. "We're going to have to find out. It won't be easy. But even so, the first step must be to get out of here. We're lucky to have a chance, but it won't last. We're a jump ahead of Dr. Schultz; if he knew what we know, he wouldn't leave us alone in here another night. And he's sure to find out soon."

"Another thing to worry about," Jenner said. "If we do get away, when he finds we're gone—won't he figure out how we did it? And won't he realize that we must have learned to read?"

"Probably."

"And then what? What will happen when he announces that there's a group of civilized rats roaming loose—rats that can read, and think, and figure things out?"

I said: "Let's wait until we're free before we worry about that."

But Jenner was right. It was a thing to worry about, and maybe it still is.

The next day was terrible. I kept expecting to hear Dr. Schultz say: "Who took my screwdriver?" And then to hear Julie add: "My thread is missing, too." That could have happened and set them to thinking—but it didn't, and that night, an hour after Julie, George, and Dr. Schultz left the laboratory, we were out of our cages and gathered, the whole group of us, before the mouse cabinet. Justin opened its doors, unlatched their cages, and the mice came out. They looked very small and frightened, but one strode bravely forward.

"You are Nicodemus?" he said to me. "I'm Jonathan. Thank you for taking us out with you."

"We're not out yet," I said, "but you're welcome."

We had no time for chatting. The light coming in the windows was turning gray; in less than an hour it would be dark, and we would need light to figure out how to open the screen at the end of the shaft.

We went to the opening in the baseboard.

"Justin," I said, "take the lead. Roll up the thread as you go. I'll bring up in the rear. No noise. There's sure to be somebody awake somewhere in the building.

We don't want them to hear us." I did not want to leave the thread where it might be found: the more I thought about it, the more I felt sure Dr. Schultz would try to track us down, for quite a few reasons.

Justin lifted the grid, pushed open the sliding panel, and one by one we went through. As I watched the others go ahead of me, I noticed for the first time that one of the mice was white. Then I went in myself, closing the grid behind me and pushing the panel half shut again, its normal position.

With Justin leading the way, we moved through the dark passage quickly and easily. In only fifteen or twenty minutes we had reached the end of the thread; then, as Justin had told us it would, the shaft widened; we could hear the whir of the machine ahead, and almost immediately we saw a square of gray daylight. We had reached the end of the shaft, and there a terrible thing happened.

Justin—you will recall—had told us that the machine, the pump that pulled air through the shaft, had switched from low speed to high when he had first explored through there. So we were forewarned. The trouble was, the forewarning was no use at all, not so far as the mice were concerned.

We were approaching the lighted square of the opening when the roar began. The blast of air came like a sudden whistling gale; it took my breath and flattened my ears against my head, and I closed my eyes instinctively. I was still in the rear, and when I opened my eyes again I saw one of the mice sliding past me, clawing uselessly with his small nails at the smooth metal beneath him. Another followed him, and still another, as one by

one they were blown backward into the dark maze of
tunnels we had just left. I braced myself in the corner
of the shaft and grabbed at one as he slid by. It was the
white mouse. I caught him by one leg, pulled him around
behind me and held on. Another blew face-on into the
rat ahead of me and stopped there—it was Jonathan,
who had been near the lead. But the rest were lost, six
in all. They were simply too light; they blew away like
dead leaves, and we never saw them again.

In another minute the roar stopped, the rush of air
slowed from a gale to a breeze, and we were able to go
forward again.

I said to the white mouse: "You'd better hold on to
me. That might happen again."

He looked at me in dismay. "But what about the
others? Six are lost! I've got to go back and look for
them."

Jonathan quickly joined him: "I'll go with you."

"No," I said. "That would be useless and foolish. You
have no idea which shaft they were blown into, nor
even if they all went the same way. And if you should
find them—how would you find your way out again?
And suppose the wind comes again? Then there would

be eight lost instead of six."

The wind did come again, half a dozen times more, while we worked with the screwdriver to pry open the screen. Each time we had to stop work and hang on. The two mice clung to the screen itself; some of us braced ourselves behind them, in case they should slip. And Justin, taking the thread with him as a guide-line, went back to search for the other six. He explored shaft after shaft to the end of the spool, calling softly as he went—but it was futile. To this day we don't know what became of those six mice. They may have found their way out eventually, or they may have died in there. We left an opening in the screen for them, just in case.

The screen. It was heavy wire, with holes about the size of an acorn, and it was set in a steel frame. We pried and hammered at it with the screwdriver, but we could not move it. It was fastened on the outside—we couldn't see how. Finally the white mouse had an idea.

"Push the screwdriver through the wire near the bottom," he said, "and pry up," We did, and the wire bent a fraction of an inch. We did it again, prying down, then left, then right. The hole in the wire grew slowly bigger, until the white mouse said: "I think that's enough." He climbed to the small opening and by squirming and twisting, he got through. Jonathan fol-lowed him; they both fell out of sight, but in a minute Jonathan's head came back in view on the outside.

"It's a sliding bolt," he said. "We're working on it." Inside we could hear the faint rasping as the two mice tugged on the bolt handle, working it back. Then the crack at the base of the screen widened; we pushed it open, and we were standing on the roof of Nimh, free.

The Boniface Estate

Mrs. Frisby said: "Jonathan and Mr. Ages got the screen open."

"Yes," Nicodemus said, "and without them I doubt that we could have done it. The steel frame was strong, the bolt was secure, and the wire so stiff we could not have bent it enough for one of us to go through. So we were glad they were with us and asked them if they would, after all, like to stay with us. Since there were only two of them, they said they would, for the time being at least."

And now began a journey that was to last, with some

interruptions, for almost two years. Parts of it were pleasant (it was a joyful feeling, at first, just to be free again and to get those laboratory collars off), and parts of it were terrible. I have made notes about all of it, and if the time ever comes when rats publish books of their own, I intend to write a book about it. It would be a long book, full of trouble and danger, too much to tell now. It was in one of the dangerous times that I lost my eye and got the scar you see on my face.

But we did have some happy times, and some pieces of great good luck, two in particular, that help to explain how we got here and what our plans are now.

It was early summer when we got out. We had known that beforehand—we could tell by the lateness of the light through the windows, though it was dark when we finally stood on the roof. We had no trouble getting down the side of the building, however. There were downspouts in the corners with plenty of toeholds (we dropped the screwdriver and the spool of thread into one of these); a little lower there was ivy; we were all good climbers, and there was moonlight to see by. In less than fifteen minutes we were on the ground. Staying in the darkest shadows, under the bushes when we could, we sped away from Nimh, not knowing or caring at first what direction we were going. Nobody saw us.

During the next few weeks we lived as we could. We had, in a way, to learn all over again how to get along, for although the world outside the laboratory was the same, we ourselves were different. We were, a couple of times, reduced to eating from dumps and garbage cans. But knowing how to read, we quickly learned to recognize signs on buildings: Groceries, Supermarket, Meats & Vegetables, for instance, let us know that there was food inside for the taking. And once inside a supermarket at night (they always leave a few lights on) we could even read the signs on the wall directing us to Section 8 for Dairy Products (cheese), Section 3 for Baked Goods, and so on. In the country there were barns and siloes stocked with grain and corn, and chicken houses full of eggs.

Occasionally we came upon other rats, and a few times we talked with them, but not for long. Because after just a few words they would begin to look at us strangely, and edge away. Somehow they could tell that we were different. I think we even looked different; either the diet or the injections at Nimh had made us bigger and stronger than other rats, and all the strange rats we saw looked, to us, surprisingly weak and puny. So we were set apart from even our own kind.

It was while we were in the country that we had our first important stroke of luck. We had just about decided, after nearly four months of freedom and constant roving, to find a place to settle down—if not permanently, at least for the winter. We thought that it should be in the country, but not too far from a town, so that we would have access to grocery stores as well as barns and gardens.

(It was about this time, too, that I began to wonder, and worry somewhat, about the fact that whatever we ate, whatever we needed, must always be stolen. Rats had always lived that way. And yet—why? I talked to some of the others about this. It was the beginning of a discontent and an idea that kept growing, although slowly.)

The season was autumn. We were walking one evening down a winding country road. We never walked really *on* the road, but along the edge, so that we could vanish into the bushes or a ditch if anyone came along. You can imagine that twenty rats and two mice traveling in procession would cause some comment, and we did not want that.

As we walked, we reached a very high fence of wrought iron, the kind that looks like a row of black iron spears fastened together, with pointed tops—an expensive fence, surrounding a large estate with a big, expensive-looking house in the middle, and well kept grounds and gardens. We walked along past this fence until we reached a gate.

"There's nobody living in there," said Justin.

"How do you know?"

"The gate's padlocked. And look. Dead weeds standing outside of it, not even bent. Nobody's driven in here for a while."

The house had a quiet, deserted look. There was a mail box in front, hanging open, empty.

"I wonder if we could get in," Jenner said.

"Why should we?"

"It's a big place. It would have a big pantry, big cupboard, big freezer. If it's as empty as it looks . . ."

We turned into the grounds, moving cautiously, and from beneath some bushes we watched the windows. As dusk fell, lights came on in several of them, both upstairs and down.

Jenner said: "That's supposed to make us *think* there's someone there."

"Yes," said Justin, "but there isn't. I could see one of the lamps when it came on. There was nobody near it. And they all came on at the same time."

"Automatic switches. To keep burglars away."

"Well, they're not keeping me away," said Justin. He ran to the house, climbed to one of the windowsills, and looked in. He tried another. Then he came back. "Nobody," he said.

So we went in. We found a small window in the back with a cracked pane, knocked out one corner of the glass, and climbed through. At first, we planned just to look for food. We found it, too, enough to last us for a year or more. As Jenner had predicted, there was a big freezer, well stocked—bread, meat, vegetables, everything—and a whole room full of shelves covered with canned food. The cans baffled us at first, as they had in the grocery stores. We could read what was in them, but we couldn't get it out. Then Arthur found a machine on the kitchen counter. He read the instructions on the side of it: Slide can under cutter and press switch. We tried it. The can turned slowly around in the machine, and when we pulled it out, the top had been cut free. I'll always remember what was in that first can—clam chowder, delicious.

After we had eaten, we wandered around the house. It was a rich man's mansion, with beautiful furniture and fine rugs and carpeting on the floor. There was a crystal chandelier in the dining room, and a big stone fireplace in the living room.

But the greatest treasure of all, for us, was in the study. This was a large rectangular room, with walnut paneling, a walnut desk, leather chairs, and walls lined to the ceiling with books. Thousands of books, about every subject you could think of. There were shelves of paper-backs; there were encyclopedias, histories, novels, phi-losophies, and textbooks of physics, chemistry, electrical engineeering, and others, more than I can name. Luckily, there was even one of those small ladders-on-wheels they use in some libraries to get to the top shelves.

Well, we fell on those books with even more appetite than on the food, and in the end, we moved into the house and stayed all winter. We could do that, it turned out, without much fear of discovery. We learned that from some newspaper cuttings I found on the desk in the study: They were about a wedding, and most of them showed pictures of a newly married couple leaving a house to begin their honeymoon. The groom was a Mr. Gordon Boniface—"heir to the Gould-Stetson fortune" —and the house they were leaving was the house we were in. According to the clippings, they were going on a trip all the way around the world. They were coming back to the Boniface Estate in May. Until then, it was our estate.

Oh, there was a caretaker-gardener who came three times a week, and once in a while he would check the house in a cursory sort of way. That is, he would unlock the front door, glance around to see that everything looked all right, and then lock it and leave. But he didn't live there; he lived in a small house down the road. And we were expecting him when he came; we had figured out, from the way the place was kept up, the lawns mowed, leaves raked, gardens weeded and watered, that there had to be somebody working on it. So we posted a watch, saw him coming, and kept watching him all the time he was there. And we made sure, when he looked in the house, that everything *did* look all right.

This involved a certain amount of work. We had to haul all our empty tin cans and other trash at night out into a hidden place in the woods quite far from the house. We cleaned up after ourselves carefully; we learned to use the water taps and the dusting cloths we found in the kitchen closet. If the caretaker had looked more closely, in fact, he would have seen that the kitchen counters were somewhat shinier than they should have been in an empty house. But he didn't. He never even noticed the small corner of glass missing from the back window.

And all winter, far into the night, we read books and we practiced writing.

The Main Hall

There came a knock on Nicodemus's office door; it opened, and Justin and Mr. Ages entered.

"Back so soon?" said Nicodemus.

"Soon?" said Justin. "It's past noon. It's lunchtime."

"Past noon!" Mrs. Frisby stood up, remembering her children waiting at home. Down in the rats home, in the artificial light, it was hard to tell the passage of time, and she had been so engrossed in Nicodemus's story that she had not glanced at the clock.

Justin was wearing a satchel like Nicodemus's, and from it he took a small paper package. "Here's Dragon's medicine," he said, putting it on the table. He asked Mrs.

Frisby: "Did he tell you about the Toy Tinker?"

Nicodemus said: "No. I was just coming to that."

"But I can't stay to hear it now," said Mrs. Frisby. "My children will be waiting for their lunch."

A plan was worked out. Mrs. Frisby would go home to take care of her children. Nicodemus, Justin, Arthur and the other rats involved would work out the details of moving her house, which would be done that night at about eleven o'clock—"after the Fitzgibbons are asleep and we're sure Dragon is, too," said Nicodemus. Mrs. Frisby would return in mid-afternoon to the rosebush.

Mr. Ages said: "And I'm going to lie down. After making that trip with this cast, I'm tired."

"You can have your choice of rooms," said Nicodemus. "Now that Jenner and his friends are gone, we have seven empty."

"Thank you," said Mr. Ages. "Mrs. Frisby, when you return I will tell you as well as I can exactly how to put the powder in Dragon's food."

As she hurried home, Mrs. Frisby considered just how much she should tell her children about all that had happened—and all that was going to happen. She decided at that stage, at least, she would not tell them about their father's connection with the rats. Also that she would not say she had volunteered to put the sleeping powder into Dragon's bowl. That would worry them; she could tell them, perhaps, when it was safely done—when, among other things, there would be no chance for Martin to volunteer in her place.

She would tell them simply that as the owl had suggested, she had gone to the rats and asked for help.

She had found them friendly and intelligent, and a group of them were coming that night to move the house to a place where it would be safe from the plow. That would be enough. She could tell them the whole story later—when she knew it all herself.

But it was not enough. The children were skeptical at first, then intensely curious, especially Timothy (who was looking stronger and feeling more energetic, but still staying in bed, primarily because Teresea and Martin had made him).

"But why should the rats do that?" said Timothy. "We don't know them at all. Nobody does. They keep to themselves."

"Maybe it's because the owl sent me," said Mrs. Frisby, searching for an answer that would satisfy him. "They seem to be impressed by the owl."

"For that matter," said Timothy, "I don't even see why the owl wanted to help. He's no friend of ours, either."

"Maybe they thought someday we could do them a favor in return."

"Oh, Mother!" said Cynthia. "How could we ever do them a favor?"

"You forget. I did do Jeremy a favor. That's what started the whole thing."

"That, and my getting sick," said Timothy. "I wish I could get up. I'm tired of bed."

"Not yet," said Mrs. Frisby, glad to change the subject. "You must save your strength, because tonight you will have to get up for a little while, when they move the house. We must be sure you're well wrapped up and hope that the night is warm."

"It will be," said Martin. "It's turned quite hot outside."

They ate lunch.

That afternoon Mrs. Frisby told the children that she must leave them to confer again with the rats about moving the house. When she thought of the danger she would face in just a few more hours, she wanted to kiss them all goodbye. But knowing that Timothy, at least, was already suspicious, she did not dare; but told them only that they should not worry if she was a little late getting home for supper.

On her way back to the rosebush she felt quite relieved, almost cheerful. Her problem was nearly solved, and the final solution was in sight. If all went well, Timothy would be saved.

If all went well. Then the thought of what she had to do came back to her like the clanging of an alarm bell. What worried her most was not so much putting the powder into Dragon's bowl, but the fear that at the last minute she might lose her nerve and bungle it somehow. That could wreck the plan.

She looked toward the Fitzgibbons' farmhouse, and there, on the back porch, lying in the sun, was Dragon. He was watching a pair of sparrows playing in the grass halfway to the chicken yard; the tip of his tail barely twitched as he debated whether or not they were near enough to spring for. He looked very big and very dangerous.

At least he was not looking in her direction, and Mrs. Frisby hurried on to the bush, directly to the hidden entrance, and slipped inside. When she reached the

152

arched portal, Brutus was standing guard as before, but this time he greeted her politely.

"I've been expecting you," he said.

"May I go in?"

"If you'll wait just a minute, I'll get Justin." He went inside the arch and pressed a small button on the wall. Mrs. Frisby had not noticed it before.

"A doorbell," she said.

"It rings a buzzer down below. If I pushed it three times, you'd see some action."

"Action?"

"That's the alarm signal. A dozen rats would come out this door, ready to fight. All the rest, with the women and children, would be hurrying out the back door."

"I didn't know there was a back door."

"It comes out in the woods, in a blackberry bramble. It's got a longer tunnel than this one."

When Justin appeared, they went down the same hallway as before, but this time, when they reached the chamber where the elevator and the stairway led down, Justin paused.

"Nicodemus thought you might like to see our main hall—just a quick look. He said you asked about the Plan."

"I did," said Mrs. Frisby, "but he didn't tell me about it."

"It's more than just a plan now, but we're used to calling it that. If you see the main hall, you'll get an idea of what we're doing."

So instead of going down as they had before, Justin led the way across the chamber, where, as Mrs. Frisby had noticed, the tunnel continued. They walked along for what seemed like several more minutes.

"Somewhere right along here," Justin remarked, "we're entering the woods. You'll notice the tunnel runs a bit crooked. We had to bend it to go around tap roots—some as thick as fence posts."

They went on until they came to a fork in the tunnel. "Right fork leads out to the blackberry bramble," said Justin. "Left fork leads to the main hall." They took the left fork.

"Now brace yourself for a surprise."

From ahead came noises: the sound of many rats talking, a sound of hurrying and thumping and of machinery running. They stepped into a room as full of activity as a factory.

It was the biggest room Mrs. Frisby had ever seen, half the size of a house, with a ceiling and floor of hard gray rock. It was brightly lit with electric bulbs —here the large sized ones, strung unshaded—and beneath them were rats at work everywhere. Rats running electric motors that ran belts that ran small circular saws, lathes, drills, grindstones, and other tools Mrs. Frisby could not name; rats hammering, welding, cutting. But most of all, rats hauling.

There was a steady procession to and from the far end of the chamber, and each of these rats wore a harness to which was fastened a pair of large, sturdy sacks, one on each side, like a miniature pack horse. As the rats trooped in, their sacks were empty. They disappeared into a part of the room that was hidden by a high wall of wood. When they came out, the sacks were full and heavy.

As she watched, a troop of ten, their sacks bulging, went past her out the tunnel; they greeted Justin and nodded at her, but they did not pause. She noticed that just inside the entrance an electric fan whirred quietly, aiming inward, pulling fresh air into the room from somewhere out in the woods.

Mrs. Frisby stood beside Justin and gaped. She felt dizzy at the sight, the motion, the noise, and the size of the room, which must have measured twenty feet long and almost as wide.

"How could you ever dig out such a big room?" she asked.

"We didn't," said Justin. "We found it. It's a natural cave. You can see that the ceiling and floor are solid rock. That's the reason, or the main one, we chose this spot to live. Others had lived here before us. Probably, for centuries before there was a farmhouse, bears. Then wolves, then foxes, then ground hogs. We had quite a cleaning job to do, I can tell you.

"When we found it, there was a large hole, only a few feet long, leading straight in, but it was so full of sticks and leaves you could hardly see it. We closed that entrance entirely and dug another, longer and nar- rower—our back door. Then we dug our living quarters under the rosebush, and the entrance you came in. But the cave is still our chief workshop. Let's go in."

As they entered some of the rats looked up, some waved and smiled, but all quickly turned back to the work they were doing, as if they were in a hurry.

"They're all on a schedule," Justin explained, talking close to Mrs. Frisby's ear to be heard above the noise, "so they can't stop working."

One group, especially busy, was gathered around an odd-shaped object of wood and metal about a foot long. It was curved and had a point at one end; it looked, Mrs. Frisby thought, rather like the side of a small boat. Could the rats be making a boat? Then she saw that they were fastening a strong metal ring to the top of it.

Justin led her to it.

"That," he said, "is our most important invention, the key to the whole Plan. We made a pilot model last fall. We tried it out, and it worked. So now we're making three more."

"But what is it?"

"It's a plow. Nicodemus designed it himself, after reading every book he could find about farm tools. It's light and sharp, especially made to be pulled by rats. It takes eight of us to pull it—more if the turf is tough. But with it we can turn over, in a day of hard work, a patch of earth about ten by fifteen feet."

"But why? What do you need it for?"

"Come over here, and I'll show you."

He led the way to the back of the cave where the high walls stood. He opened a door and beckoned her

through. She stood in a large wooden bin; starting at her feet and rising in a slope to the wall of the cave was a small mountain of grain.

"Oats," said Justin.

He led her on, opened another door on another mountain. "Wheat," he said.

And others:

"Barley."

"Corn."

"Soy beans."

"We've been building these stockpiles for a long time," he said. "All from Mr. Fitzgibbon's barn. We now have a two-year supply for one hundred and eight rats, plus enough to plant for two crops, in case the first one fails. In there"—he gestured toward the last bin in the row—"we have boxes full of seeds. Seeds for tomatoes, beets, carrots, melons and a lot more."

All the time they stood there, the steady procession of rats continued. They entered the bins, took off their harness-sacks, filled the sacks with grain, put them on again, and left through the tunnel, out the back door. They looked, Mrs. Frisby thought, like very large ants endlessly toiling on an anthill.

Justin must have got the same impression, for he said:

"If the ants can do it, Nicodemus says, if the bees can do it, so can we."

"Do what?"

"Why, live without stealing, of course. That's the whole idea. That's the Plan."

The Toy Tinker

We left the Boniface Estate on the first of May," said Nicodemus. "We knew a lot more than when we went in. We had been there eight months."

"Then," said Justin, "we found the Toy Tinker."

They were back in Nicodemus's office; Mr. Ages, having rested, sat with them.

"Not quite yet," said Mr. Ages.

"No," said Nicodemus. "That was in late summer. When we first got out, we began searching for a place to live permanently, or at least a place where we could stay as long as we wanted. We had a pretty clear idea of what we were looking for. We had had plenty of time to talk about it, on the long winter evenings in the library between reading books."

The reading we did! We knew very little about the world, you see, and we were curious. We learned about astronomy, about electricity, biology and mathematics, about music and art. I even read quite a few books of poetry and got to like it pretty well.

But what I liked best was history. I read about the ancient Egyptians, the Greeks and Romans, and the Dark Ages, when the old civilizations fell apart and the only people who could read and write were the monks. They lived apart in monasteries. They led the simplest kind of lives, and studied and wrote; they grew their own food, built their own houses and furniture. They even made their own tools and their own paper. Reading about that, I began getting some ideas of how we might live.

Most of the books were about people; we tried to find some about rats, but there wasn't much.

We did find a few things. There were two sets of encyclopedias that had sections on rats. From them we learned that we were about the most hated animals on earth, except maybe snakes and germs.

That seemed strange to us, and unjust. Especially when we learned that some of our close cousins— squirrels, for instance, and rabbits—were well liked. But people think we spread diseases, and I suppose possibly we do, though never intentionally, and surely we never spread as many diseases as people themselves do.

Still, it seemed to us that the main reason we were

hated must be that we always lived by stealing. From the earliest times, rats lived around the edges of human cities and farms, stowed away on men's ships, gnawed holes in their floors and stole their food. Sometimes we were accused of biting human children; I didn't believe that, nor did any of us—unless it was some kind of a subnormal rat, bred in the worst of city slums. And that, of course, can happen to people, too.

Had we, then, no use at all in the world? One encyclopedia had a sentence of praise for us: "The common rat is highly valued as an experimental animal in medical research due to his toughness, intelligence, versatility and biological similarity to man." We knew quite a bit about *that* already.

But there was one book, written by a famous scientist, that had a chapter about rats. Millions of years ago, he said, rats seemed to be ahead of all the other animals, seemed to be making a civilization of their own. They were well organized and built quite complicated villages in the fields. Their descendants today are the rats known as prairie dogs.

But somehow it didn't work out. The scientist thought maybe it was because the rats' lives were too easy; while the other animals (especially the monkeys) were living in the woods and getting tougher and smarter, the prairie dogs grew soft and lazy and made no more progress. Eventually the monkeys came out of the woods, walking on their hind legs, and took over the prairies and almost everything else. It was then that the rats were driven to become scavengers and thieves, living on the fringes of a world run by men.

Still it was interesting to us that for a while, at least,

the rats had been ahead. We wondered. If they had stayed ahead, if they had gone on and developed a real civilization—what would it have been like? Would rats, too, have shed their tails and learned to walk erect? Would they have made tools? Probably, though we thought not so soon and not so many; a rat has a natural set of tools that monkeys lack: sharp, pointed teeth that never stop growing. Consider what the beavers can build with no tools but their rodent teeth.

Surely rats would have developed reading and writing, judging by the way we took to it. But what about machines? What about cars and airplanes? Maybe not airplanes. After all, monkeys, living in trees, must have felt a need to fly, must have envied the birds around them. Rats may not have that instinct.

In the same way, a rat civilization would probably never have built skyscrapers, since rats prefer to live underground. But think of the endless subways-below-subways-below-subways they would have had.

We thought and talked quite a bit about all this, and we realized that a rat civilization, if one ever did grow up, would not necessarily turn out to be anything at all like human civilization. The fact was, after eight months in the Boniface Estate, none of us was sorry to move out of it. It had given us shelter, free food, and an education, but we were never really comfortable there. Everything in it was designed for animals who looked, moved and thought differently from the way we did. Also, it was above ground, and that never felt quite natural to us.

So, when we left, we decided that our new home should be underground, preferably, if we could find it, a cave. But where? We thought hard, and studied maps and atlases—there were plenty of those in the study. Finally we reached some conclusions: To find a cave, we would have to go where there were mountains—there aren't many caves in flatlands. And for food, it would have to be near a town or better, a farm.

So we wanted to find a farm, preferably a big one, with a big barn and silos full of grain, near the mountains. We studied the maps some more, and it was Jenner, I think, who spotted this area as a good place to look. On the map, a big part of it was covered with the contour lines that show mountains, and across these were written the words, "Thorn Mountains National Forest." Beneath that, in smaller letters, it said, "Protected Wilderness Preserve." Bordering this, where the mountains turned to foothills, the map showed rolling country with quite a few roads but hardly any towns, which, we thought, ought to mean farmland.

We were right, as of course you know now. It took us two months of steady traveling to get to the Thorn Mountains National Forest, but we found it; we're under the edge of it right now. And there are plenty of caves, most of them never visited by people—because people aren't allowed to drive into a wilderness preserve. There aren't any roads in the forest, but only a few jeep trails used by rangers, and airplanes are not permitted to fly over it.

We looked at a lot of caves, some big, some small, some dry, but mostly damp. Before we chose this cave and this farm, however, we found the Toy Tinker.

It began as a sad sort of thing. We found an old man lying in the woods one morning, near one of the jeep trails not so far from here, and he was dead. We don't know what he died of; we guessed it must have been a heart attack. He was dressed in a black suit, old-fashioned in style but neat, not ragged. His hair was white, and his face looked gentle.

"I wonder who he was, and where he was going," Justin said.

"Whoever he was," Jenner said, "he wasn't supposed to be in here at all."

"We ought to bury him," I said.

So we did, not by digging a grave, but by covering him with a high mound of leaves and stones and twigs and earth. It was in gathering material for this mound that Justin made the second discovery. He was back in the bushes, out of our sight.

"Look here," he called. "I found a truck."

It was a very ancient truck, with a small round hood, but it had been lovingly polished and was wonderfully shiny. The body, which was square and large, had been rebuilt and painted red and gold. It had little windows with white curtains, and between them, lettered in gold, were signs:

THE TOY TINKER

Toys
Repairs
Hobby Kits
Model Sets
Electrical Toys
All Work Guaranteed

Obviously the truck had belonged to the old man. He was a peddler and mender of toys, the red and gold wagon was his shop and his home, and he had driven into the woods to camp for the night. It was against the law, of course, so he had concealed the truck behind some bushes, off the trail, under a big beech tree. We could see where he had made a campfire, carefully surrounding it with stones and clearing away the brush so he would not set the woods afire. Beyond the beech tree a narrow brook flowed. It was a peaceful spot.

We could see what had probably caused the old man's death: one wheel of the truck had sunk into the soft earth and was stuck. A shovel lay near it— he had been trying to dig it out. The work had been too hard for him, and he had started to go for help when he collapsed.

This much we could figure out just by looking. Then somebody said:

"Whose truck is it now?"

"It belongs to his heirs," I said.

"Whoever *they* are," said Jenner. "He may not even have any. He seems to have been alone."

"Anyway," said someone else, "how would they ever find it?"

"That's true," I said. "We don't know who he was, and if we did, we have no way of notifying anyone. So I suppose, if we want it, the truck is ours."

"Why don't we see what's in it?"

Thorn Valley

It might almost be easier to tell what *wasn't* in it,"
Nicodemus continued. "That truck was as roomy as a
small bus, and the old man hadn't wasted a square foot
of it. Not that it was cluttered; on the contrary, everything was neatly in place on its shelf, or hook, or in its
cabinet."

It took us a while to understand what a treasure we
had found. The truck contained, as you might expect, a
big stock of toys. It also contained the old man's simple
living quarters: a cot, a lamp, a work table, a folding
chair, a bucket for carrying water, a plate, pots, pans,

and so on. There was a tiny refrigerator with food in it, and some canned stuff—peas, beans, peaches, things like that.

Most of the toys—we thought at first—we had no particular use for. There were toy automobiles and trucks, windmills and merry-go-rounds, airplanes, boats and a lot of others, mostly run on batteries. It was entertaining to look at them, and some of them we even tried out; for a while the floor looked like Christmas morning.

We tired of that and explored farther into the truck. Up near the front we found several large cardboard boxes, and when we opened them we found that they were full of electric motors of assorted sizes—replacement engines for broken or worn out toys. There were dozens of them, ranging from very small, no bigger than a spool of thread, up to some so heavy we could hardly move them.

166

Then, next to these, we found the real treasure: the old man's tools. They were neatly arranged in shining rows inside a steel cabinet as big as a trunk. There were screwdrivers, saws, hammers, clamps, vises, wrenches, pliers. There were welding tools, soldering irons, and electric drills. And the beauty of it was, since they were designed for working on toys, they were nearly all miniature, easily small enough for us to handle. Yet they were themselves not toys; they were made of the finest tempered steel, like the tools of a watchmaker or a dentist.

It was Arthur who said it first:

"Do you realize what we've got here? We could open our own machine shop. With these tools and all these motors, we could make anything we wanted."

"We could," said Jenner, "except you've forgotten one thing."

"What's that?"

"We have no electricity. The old man couldn't have run these tools off batteries. The small toy motors, yes, but not the real ones, not the power tools. He had to plug into house current to use those. See, there's his extension cord on the wall."

There was a long coil of heavy black cable hanging from a hook on the wall. It had a plug on one end and a socket on the other.

Now another rat spoke up, a rat named Sullivan. He was a great friend of Arthur's, and like him, had a particular interest in engines and electricity.

"Maybe," he said, "we could plug into a house current, too."

"How?" I said. "Who'd let us?"

"Do you remember that cave we looked at the other day? The one we decided was too close to the farmhouse?"

That was the beginning of it. The end you have seen yourself. He was speaking of the cave you saw today.

We all trooped back to it and examined it more carefully. It *was* too close, or at least closer than we had planned to live to a human habitation. But then we saw the huge rosebush near the tractor shed, where, with quite a lot of digging, we could put a concealed entrance. But most important, we noticed that there was an electric light in the tractor shed.

Mr. Fitzgibbon had an underground power cable leading out from his house to the shed. We dug a tunnel to it, tapped it, and we had all the electricity we needed. Near it ran a water pipe. We tapped that, too, and we had running water. Then, a few at a time, we moved the tools and the motors from the Toy Tinker's truck to the cave. We got nearly all of them before the truck disappeared. We went back one day and it was gone—only the hole remained, where its tire had been sunk. The forest rangers must have found it and hauled it away. But they never discovered or disturbed the mound where the old man lay buried.

So we built ourselves the life you see around you. Our colony thrived and grew to one hundred and fifteen. We taught our children to read and write. We had plenty to eat, running water, electricity, a fan to draw in fresh air, an elevator, a refrigerator. Deep underground, our home stayed warm in winter and cool in summer. It was a comfortable, almost luxurious existence.

And yet all was not well. After the first burst of energy, the moving in of the machines, the digging of tunnels and rooms—after that was done, a feeling of discontent settled upon us like some creeping disease.

We were reluctant to admit it at first. We tried to ignore the feeling or to fight it off by building more things—bigger rooms, fancier furniture, carpeted hallways, things we did not really need. I was reminded of a story I had read at the Boniface Estate when I was looking for things written about rats. It was about a woman in a small town who bought a vacuum cleaner. Her name was Mrs. Jones, and up until then she, like all of her neighbors, had kept her house spotlessly clean by using a broom and a mop. But the vacuum cleaner did it faster and better, and soon Mrs. Jones was the envy of all the other housewives in town—so they bought vacuum cleaners, too.

The vacuum cleaner business was so brisk, in fact, that the company that made them opened a branch factory in the town. The factory used a lot of electricity, of course, and so did the women with their vacuum cleaners, so the local electric power company had to put up a big new plant to keep them all running. In its furnaces the power plant burned coal, and out of its chimneys black smoke poured day and night, blanketing the town with soot and making all the floors dirtier than ever. Still, by working twice as hard and twice as long, the women of the town were able to keep their floors *almost* as clean as they had been before Mrs. Jones ever bought a vacuum cleaner in the first place.

169

The story was part of a book of essays, and the reason I had read it so eagerly was that it was called "The Rat Race"—which, I learned, means a race where, no matter how fast you run, you don't get anywhere. But there was nothing in the book about rats, and I felt bad about the title because, I thought, it wasn't a rat race at all, it was a People Race, and no sensible rats would ever do anything so foolish.

And yet here we were, rats getting caught up in something a lot like the People Race, and for no good reason. And the worst thing was that even with our make-work projects, we didn't really have enough to do. Our life was too easy. I thought of what the scientist had written about our prairie dog ancestors, and I was worried.

So were many of the others. We called a meeting—indeed, a whole series of meetings, extending over more than a year. We talked and argued and considered, and we remembered our evenings in the library at the Boniface Estate when we had wondered what a rat civilization would be like. Oddly enough, Jenner, my old and best friend, took little part in these discussions; he remained rather glumly silent and seemed disinterested. But most of the others felt as I did, and slowly some things became clear; we saw our problems and we figured out, as well as we could, what to do about them.

First, we realized that finding the Toy Tinker's truck, which had seemed like such an enormous stroke of luck, had in fact led us into the very trap we should have avoided. As a result we were now stealing more than ever before: not only food, but electricity and water. Even the air we breathed was drawn in by a stolen fan, run by stolen current.

It was this, of course, that made our life so easy that it seemed pointless. We did not have enough work to do because a thief's life is always based on somebody else's work.

Second, there was always the fear, in the back of all our minds, that we might get caught. Or perhaps not caught—we took precautions against that—so much as found out. Mr. Fitzgibbon was surely aware that some of his crops were being removed. And as our group grew larger, we would have to take more and more.

Already, he had begun lining some of his grain bins with sheet metal. That didn't bother us particularly, because we knew how to get the doors open. But suppose he should take to locking them? We could cut through the locks, of course, or even through the sheet metal walls; we have the tools for that. But it would be a dead giveaway. What would Mr. Fitzgibbon think about rats who could cut through metal?

All these things we worried about and talked about and puzzled over. But we could not find any easy answer—because there was none.

There was, however, a hard answer.

I began taking long walks into the forest. I had an idea in the back of my head. Sometimes I went alone, sometimes with some of the others.

On one particular day I went with Jenner. I had not yet told him about my idea, nor did I on the morning we set out, but merely proposed a direction. We took along enough food for lunch. I remember that it was autumn, a bright, cool day; the leaves made a rustling sound when the wind blew, and some were turning yellow.

In my walks I had been exploring the jeep trails, trying to find out where they went and where they didn't go, trying to find the wildest parts of the forest, places where not even the rangers ever went.

A few times I tried asking for information. I asked two squirrels, for instance, if they knew what lay on the other side of a mountain that rose before me. But they were silly, fearful creatures; and after looking at me in surprise, they both scurried up an oak tree and scolded senselessly in loud voices, shaking their tails, until I left. I asked some chipmunks, and they were more polite. They couldn't answer my question (never having been farther than a hundred yards from where they were born!), but advised me to ask the birds—more specifically, one bird, a very old owl who was famous throughout the forest. They even told me how to find the enormous tree in which he lived.

That was the beginning of my acquaintance with the owl. He knew every tree, every trail, every stone in the forest. He was (as you know) not naturally friendly toward rats, or mice either, but when I told him about our life at Nimh, and our escape, he grew interested. Though he did not say so, I think he had already been watching some of our activities from the air in the evenings. Anyway, he was curious and listened carefully when I told him about our problems and my ideas for solving them. I have talked to him many times since.

It was he who told me about Thorn Valley.

The valley lies deep in the forest, beyond the big tree. The jeep trails do not cross it, nor even go close to it, for the mountains around it are forbidding, too steep and rocky even for jeeps, and are covered with thorny thickets. The owl told me that in all the years he had been flying, he had never seen a human being near it.

Yet the bottom of the valley is level and broad and nearly a mile long; steep cliffs wall it in all around. There are three ponds or small lakes in it, and apparently these are fed by springs, for they never dry up. On clear days, the owl said, he sometimes saw small fish swimming in them. I thought: Could rats weave fish nets or make fish hooks?

It was this valley I was looking for the day I set out with Jenner. I had careful directions from the owl; yet it took us half a day, moving briskly, to reach the base of the mountains. Then up, up, very steeply, for more than an hour—not really difficult for us, since rats are better climbers than men; also, we are shorter, so we had little trouble with the spiney underbrush. From the top of the high ridge at last we looked down, and the valley lay before us.

It was beautiful and still, a wild and lonely place. Through the green and yellow treetops below us I could see the water of one of the ponds sparkling in the sun. I got the idea that my eyes—our eyes—were the first ever to see it. Yet that was not true, for as we descended into the valley, a deer suddenly appeared in the trees ahead and went bounding off down the slope. There were wild animals there, and I wondered if they even suspected that outside these walls of mountains there were cities and roads and people.

Most of the valley floor was in forest, great spreading oak and maple trees, but near one of the ponds I saw what I had hoped to find—a large natural clearing, a glade where only coarse grass and wild flowers grew, and some clumps of black raspberry bushes. This clearing was on the far side of the valley, beyond it the mountain wall rose again, a steep slope with big out-croppings of stone—granite ledges that thrust six or ten feet out of the earth.

"We could live here," I said to Jenner.

"I suppose we could," he said. "It's a beautiful place. But it's a long way from the barn. Think how far we'd have to carry food. And no electricity."

"We could grow our own food," I said. I started to add, but didn't: and maybe, someday, make our own electricity, if we decided we wanted to.

"We don't know how. Anyway, where would we grow it?"

"Right here. It would be easy to clear away these weeds and bushes. And if we dug into that mountainside, under those rock ledges, we'd have all the cave space we wanted, dry and warm, with a good roof. There could be room enough for a thousand of us."

"There aren't a thousand of us."

"There might be, someday."

"But why? Why move? We've got a better place to live right now. We've got all the food we want. We've got electricity, and lights, and running water. I can't understand why everybody talks about changing things."

"Because everything we have is stolen."

"That's silly. Is it stealing when farmers take milk from cows, or eggs from chickens? They're just smarter than the cows and chickens, that's all. Well, people are our cows. If we're smart enough, why shouldn't we get food from them?"

"It's not the same. Farmers feed the cows and chickens and take care of them. We don't do anything for what we take. Besides, if we keep it up, we're sure to be found out."

"What then? What if we are? People have been trying to exterminate rats for centuries, but they haven't succeeded. And we're smarter than the others. What are they going to do? Dynamite us? Let them try. We'll find out where they keep the dynamite and use it on them."

"Then we'd *really* be found out. Don't you see, Jenner, if we ever did anything like that, they'd figure out who we are and what we know? Then only two things could happen. Either they'd hunt us all down and kill us, or they'd capture us and put us in a sideshow, or maybe take us back to Nimh. And this time we'd never get away."

"I don't believe any of that," Jenner said. "You've got this idea stuck in your head. We've got to start from nothing and work hard and build a rat civilization. I say, why start from nothing if you can start with everything? We've already *got* a civilization."

"No. We haven't. We're just living on the edge of somebody else's, like fleas on a dog's back. If the dog drowns, the fleas drown, too."

That was the beginning of an argument that never had a satisfactory ending. Jenner would not yield to my point of view, nor I to his. It wasn't that he was lazy and didn't want to work. He was just more cynical than the rest of us; stealing did not bother him. And he was a pessimist. He never believed that we could really make it on our own. Maybe he was right. But I, and most of the others, felt that we must at least try. If we fail—well, then I suppose we must come back here, or find some other farm. Or eventually forget all we learned and go back to stealing garbage.

So we began working out the Plan. It has been a long time coming. Three years ago this spring we started watching Mr. Fitzgibbon to learn what he did, and how he did it, to bring food out of the earth. We collected books and magazines on farming. We discovered early that in order to stop stealing we would, for a while, have to steal more than ever. We've laid up a two-year food supply, so that even if we don't succeed in growing a good crop the first year, we won't

go hungry. We've got two-thirds of it moved to Thorn Valley already, and we've dug a dry cave to store it in, under one of the big rocks. We've got seeds; we have our plows; we've cleared and cultivated part of the land near the pond; and in a few days we'll begin our first planting. We've even dug some irrigation ditches, in case there's a drought.

We have a schedule worked out, sort of a count-down, and by early June we will be out of this cave, and out of Mr. Fitzgibbon's barn, I hope forever.

Captured

Speaking of schedules and countdowns"—Mr. Ages spoke suddenly—"we've got one for this evening. It's getting late."

The clock on Nicodemus's desk said five o'clock.

"Mrs. Fitzgibbon feeds Dragon at six p.m." He spoke gently, but his voice had a chilling sound to Mrs. Frisby. They all looked at her.

"I'm ready," she said quietly, "but there are still a few minutes, and one question you have not yet answered. Why did Jonathan never tell me anything about Nimh, or any of the rest?"

Mr. Ages said: "I'll try to explain. When Nicodemus

and the others moved into the cave near the rosebush, they invited Jonathan and me to stay with them—after all, we had been with them for many months by that time— and at first we did. But after a few weeks we decided to move out. We were, you realize, different. We both felt strange, associating always and only with rats, even though they were our close and good friends. As for me, I wanted more solitude and less society; Jonathan, on the other hand, was younger than I and felt lonely.

"So we moved, at first together, to the basement of the old farmhouse where I still live. Then Jonathan met you, at a stream near the woods somewhere, I think he said . . ."

"Yes," Mrs. Frisby said, "I remember."

"From then on he worried. He didn't want to be secretive, but he didn't know how to tell you one thing. I'm sure Nicodemus has explained to you that the injections we got at Nimh had two effects. One of them was that none of us seemed to be growing any older at all—the children, yes, but not the adults. Apparently the injections had given us all a much longer life-span than even Dr. Schultz had anticipated.

"You can see why this would have been a dreadful thing for Jonathan to have to tell you. You never had the injections. That meant that while he stayed young, you would grow older, and older, and finally die. He loved you, and he could hardly stand that thought. Yet if it was distressing to him—he thought—how much more painful it would be to you! That is what he could not bring himself to tell you.

"He would have told you eventually; I know he intended to. Indeed, you would have found it out yourself, you would have seen it happening. But it was hard; he kept putting it off, and then, finally, it was too late."

"Poor Jonathan," said Mrs. Frisby. "He should have told me. I wouldn't have minded. But will my children . . ."

"Also have longer lives?" said Nicodemus. "We don't know yet. We think so, but our own children are not yet old enough to be certain. We do know they have inherited the ability to learn. They master reading almost without effort."

He stood up, took out his reading glass, and looked at the clock. But Mrs. Frisby interrupted again.

"One more thing," she said. "What happened to Jenner?"

Nicodemus said: "He left. He was against the Plan from the start. In our discussions, he tried to persuade others to oppose it, too. Only a few joined him; though there are some others who are still doubtful about it, they're going to stay with us and try it.

"The arguments stayed reasonably friendly, but the last straw, for Jenner, was when we decided to destroy the machines."

"Destroy them!"

"For two reasons. One, so that if anyone ever finds the cave, there won't be any evidence of what we've been doing—nothing but broken bits of metal, debris that will look like ordinary junk. We'll pull out our electric cable, our lights and our water pipes. We'll close up all the tunnels leading in.

"The other reason is more important. When we move to Thorn Valley, we're going to have some hard times. We know that, and we're braced for it. If this cave is still open, with the machines and lights, the carpets and running water still here, there will be a terrible temptation to give up and move back to the soft life. We want to remove that temptation.

"But when Jenner heard the decision—it was made at a meeting—he grew really angry. He denounced us all as idiots and dreamers. He stamped out of the meeting, and a few days later he left the group forever, taking six of his followers with him. We don't know where they went, but we think they will try to find someplace where they can set up a new life like this one.

"I wish them luck, but they'll have trouble. There won't be any Toy Tinker this time. They'll have to steal their machines—everything. That worries us some, because if they get caught, who knows what might happen? But there's nothing we can do about it. We're going ahead with the Plan; and once we get to Thorn Valley, I think we can stop worrying."

Justin stood up. "It's time to go." He picked up the paper with the sleeping draught in it.

Mrs. Frisby, Justin and Mr. Ages walked together up the long corridor to the rosebush.

"Remember, when you come up through the hole in the kitchen floor," Mr. Ages said, "you'll be under a cabinet. It's low, but there's room to move. Go a few steps forward, and you'll be able to see out into the room.

"Mrs. Fitzgibbon will be there, getting dinner for her family. They eat at about six. When she's got their dinner ready, she'll feed Dragon. He won't be in the kitchen, but he'll be waiting just outside the kitchen door on the porch. She doesn't let him in while she's cooking because he makes such a pest of himself, rubbring against her ankles and getting between her feet.

"If you look to your right, you'll see his bowl. It's blue, and it has the word Kitty written over and over again around the side. She'll pick it up, fill it with catfood, and put it down again in the same place.

"Then watch closely. She'll walk over to the door to let him in, and that's your chance. Her back will be toward you. She's got to walk about twenty feet—it's a big kitchen. The bowl will be about two feet away from you. Be sure the paper packet is open—then dash out, dump the powder into the food, and dash back. You don't want to be in sight when Dragon comes in. I can tell you that from experience."

"Is that how you got hurt?"

"I got there a few seconds late. I decided there was still time. I was wrong."

At the arch in the rosebush Mr. Ages left them. With his cast, he would not be able to climb through the hole to the kitchen; there was no point in his going farther.

Mrs. Frisby and Justin moved out of the rosebush and looked around them. It was still light, though the sun was low on the horizon. Straight ahead of them, perhaps two hundred feet away, stood the big white farmhouse. Dragon was already on the porch, sitting just outside the door, looking at it expectantly. To their right was the tractor shed, and beyond that was the barnyard fence and the barn itself, casting a long shadow. Behind them rose the woods and the mountains; to the left Mrs. Frisby could see the big stone in the middle of the garden, near which her children waited. As soon as her task was done, she thought, she must hurry to them and get ready for the move.

"We go under the right side of the house," Justin said quietly. "Follow me." They made their way around the edge of the yard, staying in the shadows, keeping an eye on Dragon. Justin still wore his satchel and had put the powder package in it.

There was a basement under the main part of the Fitzgibbons' house, but the big kitchen had been added later and stood on a foundation of concrete blocks, with only a crawl space beneath. As they approached this gray foundation, Mrs. Frisby saw that near the middle of it, a few inches off the ground, there was a square patch of darker gray. It was a hole, left for ventilation, and there was a screen over it. When they reached it, Justin caught hold of the screen and pulled the corner. It swung open.

"We loosened it a bit," he explained, holding it open for her. Mrs. Frisby crept through.

"Careful," he said. "It's dark. There's a drop of about a foot. Just jump. We put some straw at the bottom, so it's soft."

Holding her breath, Mrs. Frisby jumped blindly into the blackness, and felt the cushion of straw under her feet. In a moment Justin landed beside her. They were under the Fitzgibbons' kitchen.

"Now," he said softly, "look to your left. See the patch of light? That's the hole. The light comes from the kitchen. We've piled dirt up under it, so it's easy to reach. Come on."

Mrs. Frisby followed him; as they got near the bright hole she could see around her a little. They were walking across bare earth, dry and cool to the touch; overhead there were heavy wooden beams holding up the floor, and above those the floorboards themselves. Under the hole rose a small round hill of dirt. They walked up this, and then Justin whispered:

"This is as far as I can go. There's not room for me to get through. I'll wait here. Come back down as soon as you're finished. Here's the powder." He handed her the paper packet. "Remember to tear it open before you go out to Dragon's bowl. Hurry, now. I can hear Mrs. Fitzgibbon moving around. She's getting the dinner. Be careful, and good luck."

Mrs. Frisby first pushed the packet up through the hole. Then, as quietly as she could, grasping both sides, she pulled herself up and into the kitchen.

It was light there. But Mr. Ages had not been joking when he said the ceiling was low. There was less than an inch between the floor and the bottom of the cabinet, so that she could not walk properly but had to flatten herself out and crawl. She did, a few steps, and discovered that she was trembling. "Stay calm," she told herself. "Don't get panicky, or you'll do something foolish and spoil everything."

Thus admonished, she crept forward again until she was near the edge of the cabinet. She stopped. From there she could see out into the kitchen fairly well. Straight across from her stood a big white gas stove, and in front of it, putting the lid on a pot, was Mrs.

Fitzgibbon. Because the edge of the cabinet was so low, Mrs. Frisby could not see her head, but only up to her shoulders.

"There," Mrs. Fitzgibbon said, as if to herself. "The stew is done, the bread's in the oven, the table is set."

Where was the cat's bowl? Mrs. Frisby looked to her right as Mr. Ages had said. There it was, blue, with words inscribed around the side. Yet something was wrong. It was not two feet from the cabinet, but more like four or five. In the corner, where it should have been, rose four round wooden legs. She realized that she was looking at the bottom of a kitchen stool.

No matter, she thought. The extra distance is just a couple of feet. Mr. Ages had not mentioned a stool, but perhaps they moved it around. She crawled to her right, as close to the bowl as she could get without showing herself, and tore open the package.

Just as she did this Mrs. Fitzgibbon walked over from the stove. Her hand appeared, picked up the bowl, and Mrs. Frisby heard it thump on the counter over her head. A cutting sound—a can opener—the scrape of a spoon, and the bowl was back on the floor.

The strong fishy smell of catfood. Mrs. Fitzgibbon walked away.

Now.

Mrs. Frisby moved swiftly out into the room, across the open floor, holding the powder, her eyes intent only on the bowl. She was no longer trembling. She poured in the powder, which instantly dissolved in the moist catfood. Still clutching the paper, she turned and sped toward the cabinet.

With a bang, the lights went dim. The ceiling, which had somehow become curved, was filled with little round moons. Mrs. Frisby kept running, and her face struck a cold, hard wall of metal.

A voice shouted:

"Mother! Don't let Dragon in yet. I've caught a mouse."

Billy, the younger Fitzgibbon son, had been sitting on the kitchen stool, his feet up on the rung, eating berries from a colander. The colander, upside down, was now over Mrs. Frisby.

Seven Dead Rats

From a birdcage, Mrs. Frisby watched the Fitzgibbons eat dinner. There was dinner for her, too—bread-crumbs, cheese, and bits of carrot—on the floor of the cage, along with a small bowl of water. The cage had been occupied until a few months before by a yellow canary named Porgy, who had lived in it for five years and then died of old age.

To get her out from under the colander, Billy had slid a piece of carboard beneath it, pinching her foot sharply in the process, so that it hurt when she walked. She had been transferred first to a shoebox.

"Can I keep it?" Billy had asked his mother.

"What for? It's just a field mouse."

"For a pet. I like it." Billy had tried to look at Mrs. Frisby through some holes he had punched in the top of the box, but it was dark inside.

"I suppose so. For a few days. You'll have to feed it."

"I think I'll put it in Porgy's cage. I can't see it in this box. It must be hungry. It was trying to eat Dragon's food. Dumb mouse. It might have been killed."

No one had noticed the small torn piece of paper at first; then Mrs. Fitzgibbon had absently picked it up and tossed it into the wastebasket.

A few days! Mrs. Frisby felt sick. And after a few days—then what? Would they let her go? Or would Billy plead for a few more? But even if they did set her free—her children were alone; the rats were coming tonight to move her house. Why had Billy picked today, of all days, to sit on the stool? She had not the heart to eat the food that lay on the cage floor. She felt like weeping.

Paul came in for dinner, followed by his father. He looked at her in the cage.

"Why don't you let it go?" he said to Billy. "Poor little thing. It's scared to death."

"No it's not. It's just not used to the cage."

"I bet it will die."

"I bet it won't."

"You can't just put wild animals in cages. You have to catch them when they're babies."

"They do it in zoos."

"Yes, but they know more about it. Anyway, a lot

of those die, too."

"It's strange that it was in here at all," said Mrs. Fitzgibbon. "I haven't seen any signs of mice. I didn't think we had any."

They sat at the table, and Mrs. Fitzgibbon served the stew. It was a long, square-cut farm table, big enough to feed, besides the family, the four hired hands who would be working with Mr. Fitzgibbon during the planting and harvesting. The Fitzgibbons sat together around one end of it.

Mrs. Frisby's cage hung from a metal stand in the corner on the opposite side of the room, quite high up, so that the floor where she crouched was above their heads. She could watch them, looking down; but if she retreated to the far side of the cage, they could not see her, nor she them. She kept hoping that Paul would resume the argument with Billy and win it, or at least convince Mr. or Mrs. Fitzgibbon that they should let her go.

But Paul was now busy eating. So, moving quietly, she crept to the back of the cage. There was a sliding door halfway up the side, which Billy had lifted to put her in. Remembering Nicodemus's story, she looked at it, wondering if she could climb to it, if she could get it open if she did. Not now, but later, when they had left the kitchen. Maybe. But it looked quite big and heavy.

She thought about her children again. Surely, when Justin had waited a little longer, he would realize that something had gone wrong. He would go and talk to them. But what could he tell them? "Children, your mother went into the kitchen with Dragon and she hasn't come out." No. But whatever he said, they would be dreadfully frightened and worried. Poor Cynthia! Poor Timothy—poor all of them.

She had one small satisfaction. Dragon, who had been admitted after she was safely caged, had eaten his bowl of catfood greedily, sleeping powder and all, purring as he licked the last scraps from the bottom.

Billy was looking at the cage.

"There," he cried. "It walked. I saw it. I told you it was all right." He started up from his chair.

"Billy, stay in your place and eat your stew," said Mrs. Fitzgibbon. "The mouse can wait."

"Speaking of mice," said Mr. Fitzgibbon, who had driven to town that afternoon, "there was quite a stir today at Henderson's hardware store."

"About mice?"

"No, but nearly. About rats. I went in to order the new linch pin, and there was quite a group there, talking about an odd thing that had happened.

"It seems that six or seven rats got themselves electrocuted there a few days ago. Very strange. Henderson sells motors—he has a whole shelf of them. The rats, for some reason, had got on the shelf. He says it looked as if they were fooling with one of the motors, trying to move it."

"That's a new one," said Paul. "Rats stealing motors."

"They weren't really, of course. Anyway, it happened during the night; when he—Henderson—came into the shop in the morning, he tried to turn on the lights, and the fuse was blown. He found the rats all grouped around the motor. It had been left plugged

in, though it was turned off. They must have been gnawing at the insulation for some reason—at least that's what he thinks. They caused a short circuit, and all bunched together like that, the current went through them and killed the lot."

"Pretty good kind of a rat trap, I'd say," Mrs. Fitzgibbon remarked.

Mrs. Frisby was now listening to the conversation very closely. Dragon had stretched out on the floor, looking drowsy.

"Wait," said Mr. Fitzgibbon. "That's only the beginning. It seems that the local weekly was hard up for news. They heard about it and sent their reporter over."

"Fred Smith," said Mrs. Fitzgibbon.

"Yes. Fred wrote a little article about it, with a headline, MECHANIZED RATS INVADE HARDWARE STORE. Something like that. Well, it attracted more attention than he expected. The next thing they knew, believe it or not, the federal government got into it. They sent a squad over there from the Public Health Service with a truckload of equipment."

"Just on account of seven rats?" said Billy. "They should send the truck over here. We've got more than that."

"That's just what I said," Mr. Fitzgibbon went on. "And do you know? They're going to. I was joking, of course, but the man in charge of the group didn't take it as a joke at all. He wanted to know where the farm was, how far away, how many acres, what I raised, how many rats I thought there were. He acted really interested. It seems they wanted to examine the dead rats at Henderson's, but they couldn't. He'd already sent them to the town dump, and they were incinerated."

"I never heard of such a thing," said Mrs. Fitzgibbon. "All that fuss over a few dead rats."

"I have," said Paul. "And I bet I know what they're after."

"What?"

"They think the rats have rabies. They don't like to say so because it makes people panicky."

"What's rabies?" asked Billy.

"A disease," said Mr. Fitzgibbon. "A very bad one, spread by animals. You know, Paul, I think you're probably right. That would explain why the Public Health Service is in it. Epidemic control. Anyway, they're planning to check on the rats all over this area."

"Don't you remember," Paul said, "a few years ago when everybody had to lock up their dogs? And some people were shooting every dog they saw. That's why they keep it quiet until they're sure.

"And another thing. They taught us in the vet course

in school that when an animal starts acting strange, it may be a sign of rabies. Well, chewing electric wires —that's strange enough."

"And they think some rats here might be infected?" Mrs. Fitzgibbon sounded worried.

"I suppose they must," said Mr. Fitzgibbon, "though they never mentioned rabies at all."

"When are they coming?"

"Day after tomorrow, Saturday morning. The man in charge, a Doctor somebody, said they had some more checking to do in town tomorrow. They're coming with an extermination truck—cyanide gas, I think."

"I can tell them where to look," Paul said.

"Me too," said Billy. "Under the rosebush."

"That's right," said Mr. Fitzgibbon. "In fact, they'll probably want to bulldoze that bush out of there. I can do that with the big tractor."

"Bulldoze my rosebush?" said Mrs. Fitzgibbon indignantly. "They will not!"

"Look at it this way," her husband said. "I've got to get rid of those rats anyway. I'd already decided to; they're stealing too much feed—seeds, too, more all the time. If I paid an exterminator to do it, he'd charge a couple of hundred dollars. If the government will do it free, why shouldn't we let them?"

"Well," said Mrs. Fitzgibbon, still not soothed, "then you can spend the money to buy me some new rosebushes."

"That's just what I had in mind," said Mr. Fitzgibbon with a smile. "And maybe some lilacs, too." Mrs. Fitzgibbon had always wanted a lilac bush; they were her favorite shrubs.

Mrs. Frisby did not believe at all that it was rabies the men were looking for. She wished Mr. Fitzgibbon had been able to remember the name of the "Doctor somebody." And now she had another urgent reason to get out of the cage. Somehow, she had to warn Nicodemus.

Dragon slept on the kitchen floor.

Escape

At ten by the kitchen clock, the Fitzgibbons went to bed. Dragon was put out, the doors locked, the lights turned off. The first of these things was done by Billy, on instruction from his mother, not without some difficulty. He opened the door.

"Come on Dragon. Out."

"He won't get up."

"I never saw such a lazy cat. He gets worse every day."

Finally Dragon, protesting with only the sleepiest of whines, was picked up and deposited on the back porch. He scarcely opened his eyes.

By that time it was dark. Mrs. Frisby waited a few minutes until she was sure they were really gone and until her eyes adjusted so she could see the bars of her cage. They were vertical bars, smooth and no thicker than match sticks, which made them slippery to climb, but by turning more or less sideways, she was able to grip them fairly well. She inched her way up to the sliding door and tried to lift it.

She could tell from the first pull that it was no use. The door was stiff and it was heavy, and she could not get a good enough grip on either it or the cage wall to exert much pressure. Still she kept trying, first lifting on the middle of the door, then on one corner, then another, straining every muscle. In half an hour she admitted defeat, at least for the moment, and climbed back down to the bottom of the cage. She sat there, shaking from the effort, and thought.

Somehow, she *had* to get out. Her children, even now, would be alone in the dark house, alone at night for the first time. Martin and Teresa would be trying to reassure the younger ones; yet they themselves would be sadly frightened. What would they think? Since she had not told them about Dragon and the sleeping powder, she hoped that perhaps they would decide she had, for some reason, stayed with the rats.

But at eleven, which could not be far off (she could not read the kitchen clock in the dark), the rats would arrive to move the house. Or would they, knowing— since Justin must have told them—that she had not come out of the kitchen? She thought they would. She hoped they would, and that Justin would go with them and talk to the children and try to calm their fear. There was something about Justin, a kind of easy confidence, that would help them.

She no longer had any doubt, of course, that the rats could move her house. It was a generous thing to do, especially at a time when they were hurrying so in their Plan, their own move. And they had no idea yet of how little time they really had, of the new danger that crowded upon them. If she could only get out! She would run and warn them, and it might still not be too late.

She thought: It's a good plan and a brave one. It would be the first time in all the world that intelligent beings, besides men, had ever tried to start a real civilization of their own. They ought to have a chance. It was not right that they should be killed at the last minute. Or captured. Could it be that they—the men who were coming—were somehow connected with Nimh? Or was it more likely, as Paul had guessed, that they were only worried about rabies? She decided it didn't really matter. The result would be the same. The day after next the truck would come with its poison gas, and that would be the end of all their plans. Unless they could be warned. Wearily, she got up to climb the wall and try the door again.

She heard a noise.

It was in the kitchen, near her cage, a small scuffling on the hard linoleum floor.

"Now what kind of a bird can that be, with no wings?"

It was Justin's voice, very soft, and he was laughing. "Justin!"

"I thought you might like to come home. Your

children are asking after you."

"Are they all right?"

"They're fine. They were worried, but I told them I'd bring you back. They seemed to believe me."

"But how did you know . . ."

"That you were here? You forget. I was waiting just under the cabinet. I heard what happened. I felt like biting Billy full of holes. But as soon as I heard that you were safely in the cage, I went and told the children you were all right, but that you'd be a little late. I didn't tell them exactly why.

"Now, let's get you out."

"I tried. I couldn't open the door."

"I'll get it open. I brought along a few tools—burglar's tools, you might say—in my back pack. Should I climb up the stand? No. It looks slippery. I think I'll try the curtain."

And in a matter of seconds Justin had swarmed up a window curtain a foot away, and she heard a thump as he leaped and landed on top of the cage, which swayed under the impact. The noise was slight, but they both listened intently for a moment to see if it produced another, from upstairs. All quiet.

"Now let me look at that door." Justin climbed easily down the side of the cage.

"Oh, I hope you can get it open."

"I can," Justin said, examining it, "easily enough. But I don't think I will."

"Why not?"

"Because *you* couldn't," Justin said, "and they'll know that. So they won't be curious, let's make it open itself. As I expected, it doesn't have real hinges."

He had pulled a small metal bar out of his back pack, and was working as he talked. "Just little wire rings. Dime-store quality. Cheap, flimsy things. They're always coming apart." As he said that, one of them came apart; the door sagged and hung crazily by one corner. "There, you see? You couldn't help it if they put you in a defective cage. Come on out."

Mrs. Frisby climbed through and stood with Justin on the top of the cage.

"Now," he said, "we shinny down the stand like a fireman's pole. You go out the way you came in—under the cabinet and through the hole. I'll go out the way I came in—through the attic. I'll meet you out-side."

"Justin," Mrs. Frisby said, "there's something I've got to tell you, something I learned . . ."

"Wait till we're out," said Justin. "We've got to hurry. You see, we're having a little trouble moving your cinder block." He was off, running silently into the front of the house, from which the stairway led up two flights to the attic.

Mrs. Frisby crawled under the cabinet, searched in total darkness for the small hole, and finally felt one foot slip down. She dropped through. The square opening in the foundation was easier to find; it glowed palely ahead of her, lit with moonlight.

Justin was waiting for her as she came out of the corner of the screen. The night was warm, and a half-moon shone on the farmyard.

"Now," he said, "what was it you wanted to tell me?" He spoke seriously; he had heard the urgency in her voice. They hurried toward the garden, rounding the back porch. There, a dark heap in the moonlight, lay Dragon, no threat to anyone tonight.

"Some exterminators are coming to poison all of you." Mrs. Frisby told him, as briefly as she could, of the conversation she had heard at the Fitzgibbons' dinner table.

"Seven rats," Justin said. "Rabies. It might be. But I'll bet it was Jenner. When are the men supposed to come?"

"The day after tomorrow."

To her surprise, Justin stopped. He looked at her in admiration.

"You know," he said, "I had a feeling the first time I clapped eyes on you that you'd bring us good luck."

"*Good* luck!" She was amazed.

"Oh, its bad news. It's serious. We'll have to change our plans, and quickly. But think how much worse it would be if you hadn't overheard it. We wouldn't have had a chance."

They came into the garden.

"Is Nicodemus here?" Mrs. Frisby asked.

"No. In a few minutes I'll go and tell him. But first we need your help to get started moving your house."

"*My* help? What can I do?"

"You can talk to your neighbor. She seems to think we're stealing your cinder block. She bit Arthur in the leg."

At one end of the big stone in the middle of the garden, ten rats were digging briskly, using scoops that looked more like teaspoons than shovels, piling the earth neatly beside a hole already almost big enough to hold Mrs. Frisby's house.

But on the other side of the stone there was an impasse.

Here another ten rats stood, baffled, in a semicircle. Behind them they had deposited a jumble of equipment: odd-shaped metal bars, pulleys, wooden structures that looked like ladders, other pieces of wood that resembled small logs. But between the rats and Mrs. Frisby's front door stood a small, defiant figure. The rats, looking enormous by comparison, remained a respectful distance away from her.

"Why," said Mrs. Frisby to Justin, "it's the shrew!"

"Yes," said Justin, "and acting shrewish."

One of the rats was speaking. Mrs. Frisby recognized Arthur.

". . . but I told you, ma'am, we *do* have Mrs. Frisby's

permission. She *wants* us to move her house. Ask the children. Call them out."

"Don't tell me that. What have you done with Mrs. Frisby? It's a good thing the children haven't heard you. They'd be frightened half to death! If Mrs. Frisby wanted you to move her house, she'd be here."

"It's all right," called Mrs. Frisby, running forward. "I'm here."

"Mrs. Frisby!" said the shrew. "You're just in time. I heard a noise, and came out and found these— *creatures*—trying to dig up your house."

"I tried to explain it to her," said Arthur. "But she won't believe me."

"I certainly won't," said the shrew. "He said you *asked* him to dig up your house. Thieving rats!"

"It's true," Mrs. Frisby said. "I did ask them, and they said they would. It's very kind of them."

"Kind?" said the shrew. "Great hulking beasts. What do you mean?"

It took several more minutes of reassurance by Mrs. Frisby before the shrew grudgingly moved aside, still muttering warnings. "I wouldn't trust them. How do you know they'll do what they say?" That, of course, Mrs. Frisby could not explain to her.

The rats now commenced to dig busily at the dirt on top of and around Mrs. Frisby's cinder block. Justin said: "I've got to go and talk to Nicodemus. You'd better get the children out." Mrs. Frisby hurried into her house.

She found them waiting in the living room, unaware of the small crisis that had been taking place outside. As Justin had said, they did not seem worried.

"We were scared at first," Teresa said. "But then one of the rats came to see us. He couldn't come in, but he called to us, and we came out, Martin and I. He said his name was Justin. Have you met him? He's *very* nice."

"I've met him," said Mrs. Frisby. "Now we'd better go outside. They're getting ready to move the house."

"I'm ready," said Timothy. "I'm all wrapped up like a scarecrow."

Martin and Teresa had taken pieces of warm cloth from the bed and tied them around him. Mrs. Frisby could not see him in the dark, but when she touched him she found they had even tied a piece like a bonnet around his head and ears.

"Good," she said. "And we're lucky—it's a warm night, and dry."

They went up the small tunnel to the garden and watched in the moonlight from a hillock a few feet away. The rats had finished digging the new hole, and all twenty of them were working near the house. It was a sight to see.

As soon as the earth had been cleared from the top and sides of the cinder block, so that it lay fully exposed in its hole, all of the rats turned to the pile of equipment. Under Arthur's direction the ladder-like structures became a scaffolding—four small towers standing one near each corner of the block. Across the tops of these the rats fastened strong, light bars of metal, probably, Mrs. Frisby thought, from the Toy Tinker's truck.

From these bars they now hung pulleys wound with strong, thin cord, and at the ends of the cords they fastened hooks, which they slipped into the oval-shaped holes in the block and pulled taut. Five strong rats stood by each cord. One of them, Mrs. Frisby noticed, was bigger than the rest: her friend Brutus.

"Heave!" called Arthur.

The twenty rats strained on the cords, and the block rose an inch. Each rat stepped back a pace.

"Heave!" Another inch.

Slowly, the heavy block rose from the hole until it hung two inches above level ground.

"Steady," said Arthur. "Get the rollers."

Eight rats, two from each group, ran to the round pieces of wood Mrs. Frisby had noticed earlier; these resembled sawed-up pieces of broom handle, each about a foot long.

Two rats to a roller, they slipped four of these under the cinder block so that they lay athwart the hole, like bars across a window.

"Lower away," said Arthur, and the cinder block came to rest gently on the rollers.

"Let's see how it rolls."

They slipped the ropes free of the pulleys and re-hooked two of them to the front of the block. Nine rats now manned each rope; two stayed behind, watching the rollers.

"Heave!"

The rollers turned and the heavy block slid forward easily, like a truck on wheels, in the direction of the new hole. When it moved off the hindmost of the rollers, as it did every few inches, the two rats in the rear would quickly pick that one up and replace it under the front of the block.

Almost like a game of leap-frog, Mrs. Frisby thought. But a well-rehearsed game; the rats had planned carefully; they knew exactly what they were doing; they moved with precision and never wasted a motion.

Within a very few minutes the first of the rollers lay across the new hole; then the second, and finally all four. The block was poised and in position; the hole was exactly the right size and shape. The rats had even dug out a new pantry-hole in one corner, and carved out the small tunnel that would connect the two rooms of the house.

The towers and the pulleys were put up again, and the whole process of lifting and lowering was done in reverse; the rollers were pulled away and the block was eased slowly into its new home.

"It's done!" cried Mrs. Frisby. She felt like applauding.

"Not quite yet," said Arthur over his shoulder. To the other rats he said: "Get the shovels and the backpacks."

Pausing a moment to rest, he explained to Mrs. Frisby: "We're going to cover it with turf, and then we've got to fill up the old hole with the dirt from the new one, or Mr. Fitzgibbon will wonder who's been digging up his garden. Also, we've still to dig you an entrance hole."

In her excitement Mrs. Frisby had forgotten this small detail. She could not get into her house. Now she watched in awe as Arthur and Brutus, using two small, sharp, long-handled shovels, dug the narrow tunnel down to her living room. It took them somewhat less than five minutes. It had taken her all day to dig the other one.

"Now," said Arthur, "you can put your children to bed. We'll take care of the rest."

At the Meeting

Mrs. Frisby slept well and soundly, the day just
finished having been the longest and hardest she had
ever known.

She awoke in the morning with a smile. Her house
was warm, and it was safe at last. Her children slept
peacefully beside her; Timothy's breathing was quiet
and easy. They could stay in the house, now, as long
as they needed to. On some warm day later in the
spring, when Timothy was strong again, they would
move to the summer house down by the brook. Another nice thing, she thought—when they left the house
she would close up the entrance tunnel so that no one

could find it; undisturbed by the plow, it would be ready and waiting for them in the fall. It could be theirs forever, thanks to the rats.

The rats! In her half-dreaming state she had forgotten. They were in terrible danger. What would they do? She felt as if she ought to go and offer to help them. But help how? She could think of nothing she could do.

At that moment she heard a voice calling her name from above.

"Mrs. Frisby."

She left the bed and went to the bottom of the entrance hole.

"Yes? Who's calling?"

"It's me, Brutus. Can you come up?"

Mrs. Frisby climbed up and out her front door, blinking in the early morning sunlight.

"Nicodemus wants to know if you can come with me. He's having a meeting."

"Just let me wake the children and tell them."

Two minutes later she was walking with Brutus toward the rosebush.

"What does Nicodemus want?"

"It's about the men. Justin told us last night. Nicodemus thinks they may be from Nimh. He wants to ask you more about what Mr. Fitzgibbon said."

That morning there were two rats on sentry duty—one just inside the entrance to the rosebush, watching Mr. Fitzgibbon's house, another at the arch where Brutus had stood. All of the rest were gathered in the large assembly room Mrs. Frisby had seen when she got off the elevator. Nicodemus, Justin, Arthur and

two other rats sat on the raised platform at the end. The rest sat facing them, filling every square inch of floor space except for an aisle up the center.

Mrs. Frisby had never seen so many rats. Even the young ones were present; she spotted Isabella, staring up at the platform with wide, round eyes. Some of the mothers held small babies at their sides. Most of them looked anxious; there was an air of tension, but none of panic.

Brutus led her up the center aisle to the raised platform. There was a table on it, covered with papers, and one vacant space, where a chair had been placed for Mrs. Frisby. The rats waited in complete silence while she sat down.

Then Nicodemus said, quite formally: "Justin has told us all that happened. Mrs. Frisby, it seems you have more than repaid us for the help we gave you in moving your house. Just as your husband did once, you have saved us from a disaster: Death or capture—we do not yet know which."

Justin gave her a wink. "Mrs. Frisby had a taste of capture herself last night."

"Would you tell us, as well as you can remember it, word for word what Mr. Fitzgibbon said—about the rats, about the men who were at the store?"

"As well as I can remember it." Mrs. Frisby's voice sounded small in the big room. "Mr. Fitzgibbon said a strange thing had happened in the hardware store— Henderson's, he called it."

Her memory was good; she had listened with great care to what Mr. Fitzgibbon had said, and she was able to recall the whole conversation word for word. The rats sat quietly while she told it.

Then Nicodemus went back over it, asking questions.

"You say that Mr. Fitzgibbon said six or seven rats. Did he ever say which number it really was?"

"No. I don't think he paid much attention to the number."

"Jenner's group was seven," said Justin. "But it could be a coincidence."

"Did he say how far away the town was where this happened? Or did he name it?"

"No. But it must not be very far. He'd been there and back that day."

"Did anyone see his car go out?" Nicodemus asked the others.

"I heard it," Brutus said. "I was on duty. It went after lunch."

"And he was back by dinner. But which direction? If we knew, we might send someone. You see," Nicodemus explained to Mrs. Frisby, "we need to know who those men are. If they're from Nimh, things are much worse for us."

"We'd never make it," said Arthur. "Driving at, say, forty or fifty miles an hour, Mr. Fitzgibbon might have gone fifteen or twenty miles in any direction, and returned easily the same afternoon. On the map"— there was a road map on the table—"you can see it could have been any one of half a dozen small towns. And each of them might have a hardware store."

"You're right, of course," said Nicodemus. "Without the name, that idea is hopeless." He turned back to Mrs. Frisby. "Mr. Fitzgibbon said the rats were grouped around the motor 'as if they were trying to move it'?"

"That's what he said the store owner told him. He didn't see it himself."

"And that the motor was plugged in."

"'Had been left plugged in'," Mrs. Frisby quoted.

"But we don't know who plugged it in."

"I got the impression," Mrs. Frisby said, "from the way he said it, that the storeowner had left it plugged in. But I'm not sure."

"That would make sense," Arthur said. "If it was Jenner, and if they had plugged it in themselves, they'd have known better than to try to move it. So they must not have realized. It was probably pretty dark in the store."

"Poor Jenner," said Nicodemus. "I wish he had stayed with us."

"It will be poor *us*," said one of the rats at the table (Mrs. Frisby did not know his name), "if we don't get on with this."

"He did not mention the doctor's name," Nicodemus said. "Did he say even a word about what he looked like?"

"No."

"Did he describe the truck at all?"

"No. Only that it was full of equipment."

"Are you sure about the headline in the local paper: 'Mechanized Rats Invade Hardware Store'?"

"I'm sure that's what Mr. Fitzgibbon said it was. But I don't think he saw it. He didn't say so."

"In a way, that's the most puzzling thing about the whole story," Nicodemus said.

"Why is that?" asked Justin.

"Because the headline doesn't really fit the facts. You don't call a bunch of dead rats mechanized just because you find them on a shelf near a motor."

"Maybe not," said the nameless rat. "But then why did the newspaper say that?"

"I'm wondering," Nicodemus said, "if perhaps there wasn't more to the story. Some stronger reason to think they were really taking the motor away, or that they knew how to use it."

"Maybe some other motors had been stolen," Justin said. "Or some tools. That would make them seem mechanized."

"It would," said Nicodemus. "And it would explain what the doctor meant when he said they had more checking to do in town."

"They're looking for the things that were missing," Arthur said, sounding suddenly worried. "They're looking for Jenner's headquarters. And if they find it . . ."

"We're just guessing, of course," Nicodemus said. "But it's a possibility."

"And a bad one."

"It means," Nicodemus continued, "that we have no choice. We've got to assume they're from Nimh. We've also got to assume that by now they may have found Jenner's headquarters—whatever cave or cavern they were using."

"And," said Justin, "that now they're looking for us."

"Why for us?" asked one of the rats. "Why wouldn't they think Jenner's group are the only ones?"

"They might," Nicodemus admitted, "but I don't think so. After all, they know that there were twenty of us originally. Why should there be only seven now? And we already know that they're coming out here—in quite a hurry at that. So if they're from Nimh, obviously they *are* looking for us."

"I think," said Arthur, "that we've got to make some plans, and quickly."

"I agree," said Nicodemus. "It's a new situation, and a tricky one. We won't be able to do everything we hoped to. There isn't time. And somehow we have to convince the exterminators, when they come, that we aren't more of the mechanized rats they're looking for.

"We won't be able to move any more food to Thorn Valley," Nicodemus continued. "We'll have to get along on what we've already got stored there—about an eighteen-month supply, if we're careful. The seeds, I believe, are already moved."

"Yes," said Arthur. "The last load went yesterday."

"So with luck, we'll have our own first crops this summer and fall.

"We won't have time to destroy the motors, or the books, or the furniture as we planned. Instead, we'll move everything to the cave. And then we'll seal off all entrances to the cave as if it had never existed."

"That can be done," Arthur said.

"But there's more: We've got to pull all the wires and lights from the tunnel—they're likely to dig it up. And the carpet. We've got to tear down the arch.

"Then, when all that's done, when everything is hidden in the cave, we'll fill in the stairway and the elevator shaft. We'll seal off everything except the upper storage room and the tunnels leading in the front and out the back.

"When they dig, let them find that room. It's as big as an ordinary rat hole.

"Justin, tonight, take a group of a dozen or so. Go to the Fitzgibbons' garbage can. Bring back a load of the worst-smelling garbage you can find. The storage room is going to become an ordinary, typical rat hole, not in the least mechanized or civilized."

Nicodemus turned to Arthur: "What do you think?"

"I think we can do it all. We won't get much sleep, though."

Justin said: "But there's one more thing. Won't they think it's odd—especially if they're from Nimh—finding just an empty hole?"

Nicodemus said: "I was coming to that." He sounded suddenly very tired. "Tomorrow morning, as soon as it's light, the main group leaves for Thorn Valley. But some of us will have to stay behind. As Justin says, if they find just an empty hole, they're sure to be suspicious, and they'll keep on digging. So when they come with their gas truck, they've got to find some rats here. A rear guard. I'd say at least ten."

Mrs. Frisby walked slowly home, keeping to the edge of the woods, keeping out of sight.

Justin had instantly volunteered for the rear guard. Brutus was second, and behind him, eight more; there were fifty more waiting behind them. "Enough, enough," said Nicodemus. Isabella, in tears, had run forward. "I *want* to stay, *please*," she had pleaded, looking despairingly at Justin. "No children," said Nicodemus, and her mother led her away, still weeping.

Those ten, the ten who would remain, did not face certain death, nor certain capture. The exterminators (they presumed) would make noise, especially if they cleared away the rosebush. The rats would be alerted. When the men pumped gas (as expected) into the hole, the pump would also make a noise; the air below would move as the gas flowed in. When they felt that, the rats would scramble out the back exit, past the sealed-off cave, emerge as noisily as possible in the blackberry bramble—indeed, show themselves—and dash off into the woods.

"But won't they block the rear exit?"

"Or put a net over it?"

"We'll give them another rear exit to block," Arthur had said cryptically. "One that's easier to find."

"Mother, why are you so quiet?" asked Teresa. They were sitting down to dinner for the first time in their newly moved house. "You seem sad."

"I suppose I am," Mrs. Frisby said. "Because the

214

rats are all going away."

"But that's no reason. It's true, they moved our house, and that was nice of them. But we didn't really *know* them."

"I was getting to know them pretty well."

"Where are they going?" Cynthia asked.

"To a new home, a long way away."

"When?"

"Tomorrow morning."

"Will you go to see them off?"

"I think I will."

"But why are they moving away?" asked Timothy.

"Because they want to," said Mrs. Frisby. Someday soon she would tell them the whole story. But not that night.

The Doctor

The next morning Mr. Fitzgibbon started the larger of his two tractors, the huge one he kept in the barn, the one that pulled the combine in the fall harvest. With help from Paul and Billy, he bolted the big bulldozer blade to the front of it, rumbled it up through the barnyard gate and stopped it near the rosebush.

"We'll wait until they come," he said, turning off the engine.

Mrs. Frisby could not bear to watch; and yet, even more, she could not bear not to watch. She knew there was nothing to be gained by it, nothing she could do. Yet how could she stay at home when the ten rats, including Justin and Brutus, were waiting bravely underground? She could not.

She thought at first of her watch-hole in the corner post. Then she decided against it. Nearer to the rosebush, on the edge of the woods, stood a hickory tree, its scaly bark like a ladder inviting her to climb. Ten feet up on this tree a large branch jutted straight out. On this branch, up close to the trunk, she had a vantage point from which, herself unseen, she could look down on the rosebush and also see into the woods to a blackberry bramble where, though she had never been in it, she was sure the rats' rear exit must be hidden. She settled down to wait. It was a chilly morning, with a damp breeze and a gray mist that blew by in patches.

Somewhere near the middle of the morning a square white truck came into the driveway. It went first to the house. A man in a white coverall uniform climbed out and knocked on the Fitzgibbons' door; it was too far away for Mrs. Frisby to hear the knock, or to hear what the man said when Mrs. Fitzgibbon came out on the porch. But ten seconds later Billy ran from the house to the barn, where Mr. Fitzgibbon was working.

The man returned to the truck and waited, standing outside the open cab door. Through the windshield she could see that two more men sat in the front seat, and that one of them wore horn-rimmed glasses.

Now Mr. Fitzgibbon approached the truck, Billy dancing beside him, apparently in some excitement. There was a conference, none of which Mrs. Frisby could hear, accompanied by gestures toward the rose-bush and the waiting bulldozer. The man in white climbed back into the driver's seat and drove the truck across the grass. He backed it up beside the bulldozer, stopping perhaps ten feet from the bush. Mrs. Frisby stared at it. If there was anything printed on it, it must be on the other side, away from her. Then three men climbed out, and she could hear what they said.

"It's a big one, all right," said one of the men. "And look at those thorns. It's hard to see how even a rat could get in there."

The man in the horn-rims walked around the edge of the bush, examining it closely. He bent over.

"Look at this," he said. "There's the entrance hole, very neatly hidden. And look behind it—a path leading in."

He turned to Mr. Fitzgibbon, who had walked up with Billy.

"You were right. You'll need to bulldoze it. It would take us all day to hack our way in there. But cut it off just at the surface if you can. If you dig too deep and open the hole, they'll get away."

He added: "You better tell the boy to keep back. We'll be using cyanide, and it's dangerous."

Billy, after some argument, was dispatched to the

back porch, where Mrs. Fitzgibbon was also watching.

One of the men had walked around to the far side of the bush, the side near Mrs. Frisby's tree.

"Doc," he called, "here's another entrance in the bush, and there's a hole just inside it."

"Doc" was the man in the horn-rims. He was a doctor. Mrs. Frisby thought: Doctor Somebody. He was in charge.

"Can you get at it?" he asked.

"Not very well. Too many thorns."

The man who was a doctor walked around and looked at it. "No," he said. "Anyway, that would be the escape hatch. We'll find the main hole nearer the middle of the bush."

He turned to Mr. Fitzgibbon, who had mounted the tractor. "Okay," said the doctor. "Can you push it that way—away from the shed?"

Mr. Fitzgibbon nodded, and the motor started with a roar. He pulled a lever and flexed the heavy steel blade up and down, bringing the bottom edge to rest just even with the ground. The blade was fully eight feet across. He pulled another lever; the wheels, with cleated tires as tall as windows, dug in and the blade scraped forward.

The bush fought back, then yielded angrily, snapping and crackling before the inexorable thrust of steel. A single sweep, and a third of it lay, a writhing heap of thorns, in a pile twenty feet away. The ground trembled under the wheels, and Mrs. Frisby thought of the ten rats huddled below. Supposing the weight collapsed the earth, caved in the storage room and trapped them? Another sweep, and a third. Only a thorny stubble now stood where the bush had been. On the porch Mrs. Fitzgibbon covered her eyes with her hands, and Billy cheered in excitement.

Plainly exposed were two holes—simple, round rat holes. There was no trace of the small mound nor the elegant arched entrance. Arthur had done his work thoroughly. Mrs. Frisby wondered for a moment at the second hole. Then she remembered his saying: "We'll give them another rear exit to block." Of course! They had dug another hole, most likely, she thought, just a dummy, leading nowhere.

The men in the white suits went into action. The back doors of the truck were opened and a long, flexible pipe unrolled. It looked like a fire hose, except that at the end, instead of a nozzle, there was a round plunger like a big rubber ball cut in half. One of the men donned a mask with a glass visor and a tube that ran to a pack on his back. A gas mask.

The masked man pulled the hose over to the center rat hole and pressed the plunger over it, covering it completely.

From the back of the truck the other two took a large box made of wood and wire, almost a yard wide, and placed it over the second hole. It was a cage, but half of its bottom was a trapdoor, neatly mounted on hinges. This they raised, placing the open part directly over the opening in the earth. Then they backed away, one of them holding a trip cord which would close the trapdoor after the rats were inside.

"All set?" The doctor called to the man in the mask. The mask nodded.

"Keep back, now," said the doctor to Mr. Fitzgibbon,

220

who had left his tractor to watch. He walked to the truck, reached inside, and turned a switch. Mrs. Frisby heard the soft throb of a pump.

Now.

She turned and watched the blackberry bramble in the woods. Would they hear the pump? Where were they? Oh, *let* them come out. Almost a minute passed. The men in white watched the trap. Nothing moved.

Then she saw it. Behind the bramble, half-hidden by a swirl of mist, a gray-brown shape, a rat, shaking dirt from his ears. Another. Then three more. They huddled in silence, waiting. More. How many? Ten? Seven. Only seven. Where were the other three? Still they waited.

Then, as if by agreement, they stopped waiting. They ran. All seven of them, not back into the woods to safety, but out of the woods, toward the stubble of the rosebush, toward the men. At the edge of the bush, they stopped as if in confusion, ran to the left, ran to the right, then fled back into the woods again. Now they were out of sight of the men, but not of Mrs. Frisby. Instantly they regrouped behind the blackberry bramble and charged out again—but this time in smaller numbers: first two, then three, then two again. She saw what they were up to. They were not in the least confused; they were making seven rats look like twenty rats, or forty, a steady stream of them. In the mist, in the hectic turning, running, turning, hiding, she could not tell whether or not she recognized any of them.

The men shouted:

"Look at that!"

"A pack of them!"

"How did they get out?"

"Get the nets!"

The doctor turned off the pump; the man with the hose pulled off his mask. As a new wave of rats danced along the edge of the clearing all three men ran to the truck and from it pulled long-handled nets.

But Mrs. Frisby, up on her branch, was staring at the blackberry bush again. She saw something that all of the others, including the rats, did not see. An eighth rat had come out. He emerged running, but then he stumbled; he got up and ran again, this time more slowly, circling vaguely to the right. He did not seem to know where he was going. He reached a sparse thicket of saplings almost out of her sight, and there, abruptly, he fell over on his side and lay still.

Meanwhile all three men, holding their nets low, ran across the stubble toward the parade of rats. But as they approached the parade it vanished; the rats, their purpose accomplished, melted into the misty woods, and this time they did not reappear. Mrs. Frisby watched them as they loped away swiftly in single file and disappeared from her view, back into the deep forest and up the mountainside. The rear guard was gone, bound for Thorn Valley.

But the eighth rat still lay unmoving among the saplings. And two had never come out at all.

"They're gone," said the man who had worn the mask. "They fooled us."

"What happened?" asked Mr. Fitzgibbon, standing near the truck.

"Simple enough," said the doctor. "They had two escape holes, and they used the other one." He walked back to the blackberry bramble and bent down, kicking the branches aside with his foot. "Here it is," he said. "Quite a long tunnel. One of the longest I've seen."

To the other two men he said: "Get the pick and the shovels."

For half an hour they dug, laying open a narrow trench along the tunnel. From her angle of view in the tree, Mrs. Frisby could see only the top of this trench, and not down into the bottom. Still she watched, saying to herself, perhaps, after all, there were only eight, maybe they decided that eight would be enough.

Then one of the shovels broke through into air; they had come to the rats' storage room.

"There's two of them," said one of the men, and her heart sank. Who were they? She wanted to run and look, but she did not dare.

"Careful," said the doctor. "There may still be some gas in there. Let the wind blow it out."

"Phew," said one of the men. "That's not gas, that's garbage."

"Open it up a little more," said the doctor.

One of the men wielded his shovel for another minute, and then the doctor peered in.

"Garbage," he said. "Last night's dinner. Garbage and two dead rats." Mrs. Frisby thought: He sounds disappointed.

"Only two?" said Mr. Fitzgibbon.

"Yes. It's easy to see what happened. In a hole this size there would have been a couple of dozen at least. But these two must have been up at the front, near the tunnel. They got a whiff of the gas, and it killed

223

them. But before they died, they must have warned the others. So the rest ran out."

"Warned them?" said Mr. Fitzgibbon. "Could they do that?"

"Yes," said the doctor. "They're intelligent animals. Some can do a great deal more than that." But he did not elaborate; instead he turned to one of the men. "We might as well take these two back with us."

From the truck the man produced a white paper sack and a pair of plastic gloves. He pulled the gloves on, reached into the hole and placed the two dead rats into the sack. He did this with his back to Mrs. Frisby, so that she never got even a glimpse of them.

"All right," said the doctor. "Let's close it up." They shoveled the dirt back into the trench and returned to the truck.

"You'll let me know if they have rabies?" said Mr. Fitzgibbon.

"Rabies?" said the doctor. "Yes, of course. But I doubt it. They look perfectly healthy."

Perfectly healthy, thought Mrs. Frisby sadly, except for being dead. She looked into the woods, over toward the saplings where the other rat lay. Was he, too, now dead? To her surprise, she saw that he was moving. Or was he? In the mist it was hard to tell. But something had moved.

After the truck had left Mr. Fitzgibbon stood looking at the ruin of the rosebush. He seemed vaguely puzzled and disappointed; he must be wondering, she thought, whether it had been worth it, just to exterminate two rats. He had no way of knowing, of course, that all the rest were also gone and would not return, that his grain loft was safe. In a moment he turned and walked to the house.

As soon as he was safely gone Mrs. Frisby scurried down from her tree and into the woods. On the ground she could no longer see the rat or the thicket where he lay, but she knew the direction, and she ran. Around a stump, over a mound of leaves, past a cedar tree— there were the saplings, and there lay the rat, still on his side.

It was Brutus. Beside him, futilely trying to move him, stood Mr. Ages.

She reached him, breathless from her run.

"Is he dead?"

"No. He's unconscious, but he's alive and breathing. I think he'll revive if I can just get him to swallow this." Mr. Ages indicated a small corked bottle, no bigger than a thimble, on the ground beside them.

"What is it?"

"An antidote for the poison. We thought this might happen, so we got it ready last night. He got just a little of the gas, made it this far, and then collapsed. Help me lift his head."

Mr. Ages had been unable to lift Brutus's head and the bottle at the same time. Now, with Mrs. Frisby's help, he forced open Brutus's mouth and poured in just a few drops of the smokey liquid the bottle contained. In a few seconds Brutus made a gulping noise, swallowed hard, and spoke.

"It's dark," he said. "I can't see."

"Open your eyes," said Mr. Ages.

Brutus opened them and looked around.

"I'm out," he said. "How did I get here?"

"Don't you remember?"

"No. Wait. Yes. I was in the hole. I smelled gas, an awful, choking, sweet smell. I tried to run, but I stumbled over somebody lying on the floor, and I fell down. I must have breathed some of the gas. I couldn't get up."

"And then?"

"I heard the others running past me. I couldn't see them. It was darker than night. Then one of them ran into me, and stopped. He pulled me up, and I tried to run again. But I was too dizzy. I kept falling. The other one helped me up again, and I went a few steps more. He kept pulling me, and then pushing, and somehow, finally, I got to the end of the tunnel. I saw daylight, and the air smelled better. But there was nobody else there; I thought the others must have left. So I ran a little farther, and that's all I remember."

Mrs. Frisby said: "What about the one who helped you?"

"I don't know who it was. I couldn't see, and he didn't speak at all. I suppose he was trying to hold his breath.

"When we got near the end, and I could see daylight, he gave me one last shove toward it, and then he turned back."

"He went *back?*"

"Yes. You see, there was still one rat back in there— the one I stumbled over. I think he went back to help that one."

"Whoever he was," said Mrs. Frisby, "he never came out. He died in there."

"Whoever he was," said Mr. Ages, "he was brave."

226

Epilogue

A few days later, early in the morning, the plow came through the garden. Mrs. Frisby heard the chug of the tractor and the soft scrape of the steel against the earth. She watched from just inside her front door, fearfully at first, but then with growing confidence. The owl and the rats had calculated wisely, and the nearest furrow was more than two feet from her house.

Behind the plow, in the moist and shining soil, the rudely-upturned red-brown earthworms writhed in a frenzy to rebury themselves; hopping along each furrow a flock of spring robins tried to catch them before they slid from sight. And when the plowing was done and the worms had all disappeared, either eaten or safely underground, Mr. Fitzgibbon came back with the harrow, breaking down the furrows, and turned them all up again. It was a good day for the robins.

After the harrow, for the next two days came the Fitzgibbons themselves, all four of them with hoes and bags of seeds, planting lettuce, beans, spinach, potatoes, corn and mustard greens. Mrs. Frisby and her family kept out of sight. Thoughtfully, Brutus and Arthur had dug their doorway behind a tuft of grass, so that not even Billy noticed it.

Brutus and Arthur. Mrs. Frisby did not suppose she would ever see either of them again, nor Nicodemus, nor any of the others. Brutus, after swallowing Mr. Ages' medicine and resting for half an hour, had gone on his way into the forest to join the colony in Thorn Valley. There was no talk of their coming back, unless their attempt to grow their own food should fail—and she did not believe that would happen; they were too smart. And even if they did fail, they would probably not come back to Mr. Fitzgibbon's farm.

She thought that it would be pleasant to visit them and see their new home, their small lake and their crops growing. But she had no idea where the valley was, and it would be, in any case, too long a journey for her and the children. So she could only wonder about them: Were they, at that moment, like the Fitzgibbons, planting seeds behind their own plow? Some (like Isabella's mother) might grumble about the hardness of the new life they had chosen. Yet the story of what had happened to Jenner and his friends (if it *was* Jenner and his friends), to say nothing of the destruction of their own home, would surely help to convince them that Nicodemus's ideas were right.

The Fitzgibbons finished their planting, and for a week or two all was quiet. But it would not stay that way. The crops would appear, the asparagus was ready to sprout, and for the rest of the spring and summer the garden would be too busy a place for mice to live in comfortably.

So on a day in May as warm as summer, early in the morning, Mrs. Frisby and her children laid a patchwork of sticks, grass and leaves over the top of the entrance to their cinder block house, and then carefully scraped earth over it so that it would not show. With luck, they would not have to dig a new one in the fall.

They walked to their summer house, taking half a day to do it, strolling slowly and enjoying the fine weather, stopping on the way to eat some new spring leaves of field cress, some young poke greens and a crisp, spicy mushroom that had sprouted by the edge of the woods. For their main course, a little farther on, there was a whole field of winter wheat, its kernels newly ripe and soft.

As they approached the brook, toward the big tree in the hollow of whose roots they would make their summer home, the children ran ahead, shouting and laughing. Timothy ran with them, and Mrs. Frisby was glad to see that he showed no trace of his sickness. It was an exciting time for them. In the garden they were always alone with themselves, but along the bank of the brook in summer lived five other mice families, all with children. Within a few minutes of arrival, her four had gone with a group of the others down to the water to see the tadpoles swim.

Mrs. Frisby set about the job of tidying up the house, which had acquired a carpet of dead leaves during the winter, and then bringing in a pile of soft green moss to serve as bedding for them all. The house was a roomy chamber with a pleasant, earthy smell. Its floor was hard-packed dirt, and its wooden roof was an arched intertwining of roots, above which rose the tree itself, an oak.

On her way to get the moss she saw one of her neighbors, a lady mouse named Janice who, like herself, had four children. Janice ran over to talk to her.

"You're so late getting here," she said. "We all thought something must have happened to you."

"No," said Mrs. Frisby, "we're all fine."

"But don't you live in the garden?" Janice persisted. "I should have thought you'd be afraid of the plowing."

"As a matter of fact," Mrs. Frisby explained, "they didn't plow the particular spot in the garden where we live. It's behind a boulder."

"You were lucky."

"That's true." More than that Mrs. Frisby did not

tell; she had agreed to keep a secret, and she would do as she had said.

Still, she thought after quite a long deliberation, it was probably all right to tell her children, first making *them* promise to keep it secret. They were, after all, the children of Jonathan Frisby. For all she knew, and for all Nicodemus knew, they were likely to turn out to be quite different from other mice, and they had a right to know the reason.

The following evening, therefore, when they had finished an early supper, she gathered them around her.

"Children, I have a story to tell you. A long one."

"Oh, good!" cried Cynthia. "What kind of a story?"

"A true one. About your father, and about the rats."

"How can it be about father *and* the rats?" Teresa asked.

"Because he was a friend of theirs."

"He was?" said Martin incredulously. "I never knew that."

"It was mostly before you were born."

To everyone's surprise, Timothy said, "I thought he might be. I think Mr. Ages was, too."

"How did you know that?"

"I didn't know it. I just thought it. A couple of times I saw Mr. Ages leaving their rosebush. And I knew that Father used to visit him a lot. But I never saw him near the rosebush."

Probably, Mrs. Frisby thought, because he would have been careful always to leave through the blackberry bramble, just so we would not see him.

They sat down outside the entrance to the house, and beginning at the beginning, with her first visit to

231

the rats, she told them all that she had seen and done, and all that Nicodemus had told her. It took a long time to tell it, and as she talked the sun sank low, turning the sky red and lighting the tops of the mountains, beyond which, somewhere, the rats of Nimh were living.

The children's eyes grew round when she told them about the escape from Nimh, and even rounder when she described her own capture and escape from the birdcage. But in the end the eyes of Teresa and Cynthia were filled with tears, and Martin and Timothy looked sad.

Teresa said: "But Mother, that's terrible. It must have been Justin. He saved Brutus and then went back. And he was so nice."

Mrs. Frisby said: "It may have been Justin. We can't be sure. It could have been one of the others."

Martin said: "I'm going to find out. I'm going to go to the Thorn Valley, somehow, someday."

"But it's too far. And you don't know where it is."

"No. But I'll bet Jeremy knows. Remember, he told you the rats had a clearing back in the hills. That must be in Thorn Valley." He thought about this for a minute. Then he added: "He might even fly me there on his back, the way he did you."

"But we don't know where Jeremy is, either. We don't see the crows down here," Mrs. Frisby reminded him.

"No, but in the fall, when we go back to the garden —I could find him then. If I got something shiny and put it out in the sun, he'd come to get it." Martin was growing excited at his idea. "Oh, Mother, *may* I?"

"I don't know. I doubt that the rats will want visitors from the outside."

"They wouldn't mind. After all, you helped them, and so did Father. And I wouldn't do any harm."

"It's not something we have to decide tonight," said Mrs. Frisby. "I'll think about it. And now it's late. It's time for bed."

The sun had set. They went into the house and lay down on the soft moss Mrs. Frisby had placed on the floor of their room under the roots. Outside, the brook swam quietly through the woods, and up above them the warm wind blew through the newly opened leaves of the big oak tree. They went to sleep.

KOHEN